WE TWO

WE TWO

*Couples talk about
living, loving and
working partnerships
for the '90s*

EDITED BY
Roger Housden &
Chloe Goodchild

Aquarian/Thorsons
An Imprint of HarperCollins*Publishers*

The Aquarian Press
An Imprint of HarperCollins*Publishers*
77–85 Fulham Palace Road,
Hammersmith, London W6 8JB

Published by The Aquarian Press 1992
1 3 5 7 9 10 8 6 4 2

A catalogue record for this book
is available from the British Library

ISBN 1 85538 189 3

Typeset by Harper Phototypesetters Limited
Northampton, England
Printed in Great Britain by
Woolnough Bookbinding, Irthlingborough, Northants

When men and women come together,
how much they have to abandon! Wrens
make their nests of fancy threads
and string ends, animals

abandon all their money each year.
What is that men and women leave?
Harder than wrens' doing, they have
to abandon their longing for the perfect.

The inner nest not made by instinct.
will never be quite round,
and each has to enter the nest
made by the other imperfect bird.

From *'Listening to the Koln Concert'*
by ROBERT BLY

15 per cent of the net authors' royalties will be donated to the Spectrum Incest Intervention Project in London.

CONTENTS

PREFACE

Many people today could say that they do not know of a single intimate relationship that wholeheartedly fulfils both partners. Even if such partners are known, their friends have become conditioned by the norm to expect their love to fade, or to be replaced by yet another relationship in the currently prevailing style of serial monogamy.

How do couples manage a successful relationship in a culture where there is such disillusion and suffering associated with intimacy, and such confusion over the questions of male and female roles, commitment, childrearing, fidelity, and the nature and value of love itself?

There is no easy answer to this question, although new models of intimacy are beginning to emerge in the West in response to changing social and cultural conditions; and throughout society there are individual couples who are testimony that, whatever the form, old or new, love can stand the test of time. Despite the divorce rate, as many people marry as ever before, and if it doesn't work the first time, most of them try again. The myth of romantic love is certainly as alive as ever, if not more so. How is it adapting to the changing times, though, and how is it responding to other prevailing and competing myths, such as the quest for individual self-fulfilment, more usually seen in terms of work and creative endeavours?

These are the questions this book explores, along with the broad subject of contemporary love and intimacy, through the personal stories of nine couples. The contributors have each written a chapter on their own individual experience of living with their partner. They describe the issues they find themselves most often needing to face; what they find difficult and what they find joyful; and the ordinary details of an everyday life together. Above all, they tell their own 'story' of intimate relationship – not only its history, but also the underpinning attitudes and shared assumptions they believe sustain and maintain the relationship.

Though each of them has a unique style of expression and gives a different emphasis to the various dimensions of a relationship, there are areas where a common response is evident throughout. Monogamy, for example, is considered important by all of them. No one, however, speaks of it in absolute or moral terms. Rather, it seems to be an attitude to life and their partner that has grown naturally out of the relationship's maturity. In general, there is more emphasis on fluidity – on an openness to the unknown, to the unexpected, or poetic – than on clearly defined sets of rules or agreements that are rigidly adhered to. A shared language of communication, especially in the emotional realm, is frequently mentioned as a priority; and everyone, in their own way, points to their relationship as a shared journey of the spirit.

At the same time, no one attempts to gloss over the inevitable difficulties of intimacy, to glamorize their relationship, or to offer the 'right' answers. This is not a how-to book, even though some couples mention tools of communication and other techniques which form an integral part of their life together. Our intention has been to hold a mirror to some of the pressing questions that so many people are asking themselves today in their own relationship. We have also wanted to offer a perspective of hope and possibility in an area of human life all too often associated with strife and disillusion. In essence, this is a book about men and women learning to love and to live with each other.

Though there is a case for including gay couples in a book on contemporary intimacy, we wanted specifically to address the dynamics of the man–woman relationship, which is, after all, the beauty and the beast that most people have to contend with. Gay intimacy, we believe, merits a book on its own.

All the couples are in their forties and upwards, and most have been married before. Most of them have children from previous marriages. Eileen and Michael Scott, whose marriage is the most longstanding one in the book, consciously chose not to have children at all. Frances and Christoph Greatorex, on the other hand, have raised a family together for the last 25 years. What all the couples bring to their relationship is a degree of commitment and life experience that gives them reason to see this particular relationship as the most significant one in their lives. At the same time, what they have written should not be read as if it were inscribed in tablets of stone. Their stories are windows onto a particular time and place, and they carry the spirit of that particular moment and mood. Like any living organism, a relationship grows, moves on, and changes. We hope the book will be read with this in mind.

Finally, we have ended the book with an interview with Marion Woodman on some of the themes that we asked the couples to consider. If, in addition, she speaks at some length on the work of the 'inner marriage', it is to emphasize the fact that any relationship begins and ends with oneself – perhaps the most difficult and liberating of all the reflections that face us when we share our life with another.

ROGER HOUSDEN
& CHLOE GOODCHILD

We sent the following list of themes to all contributors when they agreed to take part in the book. The questions were not intended to form a definitive or obligatory plan that they should follow, but rather to act as guidelines in the unfolding of their own story.

1   Why did you make the statement of marriage? Has the fact of marrying made a difference to your relationship, and if so, how? If you have chosen not to marry, why is this?

2   Why are you together? What are the beliefs and assumptions that you feel underpin your relationship?

3   What is the nature and quality of your commitment to your relationship? To what degree does your commitment depend upon a time factor – that is, do you see yourself committed to this relationship for life? If so, how does it differ from previous 'permanent' relationships that have since been dissolved?

4   To what degree do you see your relationship to be a monogamous one? Why is/is not monogamy important?

5   What part does sexuality play in your relationship? What are the beliefs and assumptions you hold about your sexual relationship?

6   How do you respond to feelings of jealousy and betrayal?

7   Do you ever feel any conflict between your individual sense of purpose and destiny (as expressed, for example, through your work) and your commitment to and sense of identity within your relationship?

8   Where and how does conflict arise? How do you deal with it?

9   What is it that makes your relationship alive?

10 What is your experience and understanding of love within the context of your relationship?

11 In which ways do you feel your relationship carries a spiritual dimension?

12 How do previous marriages and their children affect your relationship?

Gabrielle Roth & Robert Ansell

GABRIELLE ROTH

On Saturday I announced I was finished with men. My best friend laughed in my face and made me describe the kind of man I wanted in my life. On Sunday I met a guy named Robert at a ground-breaking ceremony. My friend suggested that he fit my description and I laughed in her face. I didn't get a chance to really talk to him but I gave him my number. On Monday I had an astrology reading.

It was clearly the astrologer who threw me over the edge of myself into the arms of the alien-other. Staring intently at my chart, he announced that, according to a unique system of his own invention, I was three planets removed from the earth. No wonder I felt so far away.

Secondly, he hoped I was an actress because, according to my chart, I was Academy Award material. Unfortunately, I was neither acting nor winning awards.

Thirdly, he told me that I would make someone an exceptional soulmate; however, my high priestess energy would never allow it.

To think that I paid this guy $175 to tell me that I was weird, in the wrong career, and would live alone for the rest of my life. Only in LA . . .

I left him and drove down Sunset Boulevard where there were billboards on both sides of the street announcing movies in which I was born to star.

I stopped at The Source, a famous LA eatery. Couples were sitting at every table. Suddenly, I felt quite alone and unable to voice the words 'table for one', so I left.

I got back into the car and cruised Sunset in search of a *café latté*. I needed something warm and reassuring. In 1977 they were as scarce as they are common today. I finally found a place that made them but the machine was broken. I took this as an omen and drove straight to the Palisades, where I was staying with friends.

Nobody was home and I was starving, the problem being that one friend was hypoglycemic and the other was on a diet. I needed something sweet, something to take away the pain I was feeling, something to fill the dark hole – not cold turkey, skim milk, cottage cheese, bread but no butter, tea but no sugar.

Precisely at this moment, Robert called. He wanted to know if I felt like hanging out at the pool of the Beverly Hills Hotel. Hanging out was not on my agenda. He asked about my astrology reading and all I could do was shake my head, which isn't the best way to communicate on the phone. He fell into my silence and asked me out to lunch. Never ask a starving woman out to lunch. You could end up spending the rest of your life with her.

The astrologer had given me a jolt. I didn't want to be the person he described, or I wanted to be and wasn't, or thought I should be and didn't know how. My mind was on the move. I didn't care that I wasn't a movie star as long as I could dress and act like one. I didn't mind being weird – at least I had no attraction to being 'normal'. But I wanted a man, the one that was meant for me.

I was tired of loving men I couldn't like. I was tired of being physically drawn and emotionally repelled, or physically repelled and mentally drawn, or any other variation on a divided self.

In this headset, with all my defenses down, a gateway opened and Robert walked through.

Years earlier, I had had a psychic reading with a silver-haired grandmother in Tulsa, Oklahoma. She saw my soul mate in her crystal ball. He was tall, slender, wore a dark suit and carried a briefcase. She told me I wouldn't meet him for several years, which I reacted to with disappointment and relief.

Now here he was and how did I know it? What made him different from all the others? It is unclear to me how he even survived my judgements. Aside from being light rather than dark, and far too quiet and conservative, he picked me up in a baby blue Cadillac convertible.

He obviously wasn't my type, but I made no move to have him take me home, so lunch turned into dinner during which we discovered a mutual friend. It was in her kitchen later that night that I realized who I was with.

Robert was leaning against her sink and I was standing about two feet in front of him telling her how we met, when I felt his energy in the small of my back. It was so strong I got caught between two words in my own sentence. In this short, sweet space, I felt his dream merge with mine and roll right off my tongue. Suddenly this very ordinary event seemed quite cosmic.

This man was different. I couldn't see the end. I could always see the end hanging around the shadows on the other side of the first kiss. Not this time. This time I knew I could really be hurt. I talked myself down from terror by reminding myself that if he left me I would write some broken-hearted poetry, do some dangerous dancing, and learn a powerful lesson. And if he stayed, I'd do the same with a different twist. So what was the fuss about?

Three days later I flew home to San Francisco and he stayed in LA to do business before returning to the east. We had spent one day apart when he magically showed up on my doorstep. My kid recognized him in the first three seconds. Most often, when I introduced my six-year-old son to the man of the moment, he'd stand up straight and shake his hand. He took one look at Robert and began jumping up and down on his bed in total bliss.

Was he acting out my true response, the one underneath the I'd-better-be-cool-cause-I'm-losing-it act?

My kid was the period on the sentence. I looked up into the

sloe-blue eyes of Mister Right. I should've known he didn't live in Marin County, but I would never have guessed that the man I was waiting for was hanging out in New Jersey.

For several months, we did the bi-coastal thing; red-eye flights every other weekend, endless phone conversations, letters, postcards, and flowers. He sent me daisies almost daily. I'm allergic to daisies but what the hell. At least we didn't have to have any of those deadly 'commitment' discussions. We simply wanted to be together; no one was resisting or begging to be convinced.

There were practical details. I lived west and he lived east and both of us had full-blown careers. First we decided to shift our realities to new territory and move to LA, only I searched all summer for a house and couldn't find one. It was September, time for school to start and I had to make a decision.

We were eating in one of those posh LA dining spots where everything is pastel and buzzing when we looked at each other and knew. He was probably fixing me one of his famous totally balanced bites with a bit of everything from his plate. I remember looking into his eyes and seeing myself in New Jersey. 'Why don't you come and live with me?' he said.

'Why don't I?' I couldn't think of any reasons. It was a test of all I had been teaching: to walk my talk and follow my feelings, even if it meant letting go of all I had worked years to build.

Goodbye to my mailing list, my Thursday morning ladies group, my three-storey redwood house with the sunken tub, my roots, my people. I left California casual for the eastern edge, fog for humidity, cars for taxis, and the Golden Gate Bridge for the New Jersey Turnpike. And I never stopped to wonder if I was totally insane.

All for this man.

The key thing for me was that I was a real person by the time we met. I had a beautiful kid, my work was deepening and expanding. I had a life. Earlier, I would disappear into my lover.

I'd make him more important – please, flatter, entertain, put him on a pedestal and wonder why I was terrified of intimacy.

I was still terrified, but I wanted to move through it, to keep going until I had nothing to hide, nothing to hold back. I was afraid to shed my skins, remove my masks, express what I felt, share my insecurity and pain. Sometimes I forgot who I was, but I never forgot who I was with. This was the person I wanted to be with for better and for worse. I wanted to grow old with this man.

And he wasn't just going to be my lover but a stepdad to my kid. They would be brothers with invisible ties tethered to the same womb, nourished in wholly different ways. And I would be a stepmother, even if I didn't like the word.

I can't say it's the easiest thing to go to bed one night the mother of one son and wake up the next day the mother of four. Being a step-parent is one step removed from the real thing and in this step there are many teachings. Suddenly there were three extra beings in my life, each a fragment of my lover fully realized.

Robert had three sons, I had one, and we had four. We were a part-time family, three of us during the week, except on Wednesdays, and six on weekends. Our dance was to expand and contract. I might have been totally overwhelmed had it not been this way.

Kids don't become friends, much less brothers, because two people fall in love. Especially when one of those kids is getting what the others want most desperately, their own father's attention, time and, according to their mother, money. Sorting out the feelings of kids from a fragmented family was my hardest task.

Every weekend we had a houseful of kids and our time together included them. No babysitters, no dates, no introductions and awkward endings. Instead, I had someone to cook with (he made a mean spaghetti), someone to stand in movie lines with, someone to follow around at museums and zoos, someone to roll my eyes at during parent/teacher meetings, someone to cuddle with while we watched TV.

I didn't want to get married. We lived together for 11 years before we married. I fear being trapped. I ask for an aisle seat on the airplane, I sit in the back of the theater, and get nervous on elevators. Robert pointed out to me after a few years of living and travelling together that I always sleep on the side of the bed closest to the door. Marriage is a closed door and in my experience it's a door that's much easier to enter than exit.

I was able to surrender almost everything, but I wanted that last door kept open. Maybe I was afraid of ruining a good thing. Our relationship has been so effortless and natural. There have been no major turbulences, no separations, no weeks of brooding silence, no betrayals, no major tensions. Some people might even consider it boring.

In our seventh year we almost had a wedding. We had the fancy celebration dinner and the honeymoon in London and Paris, but the wedding was called off. We had decided in September to get married in October and we made all the arrangements except for the ceremony. I wanted a Buddhist priest to marry us, but they were all with the Dalai Lama on that particular weekend.

I finally found a priest who had just arrived from Korea and didn't speak a word of English. He had a loft/temple in Chelsea and wanted his whole congregation to attend the ceremony, which would be in Korean of course.

We were only going to invite our kids until one of Robert's sons freaked out with a 'how-could-you-do-this-to-your-parents' kind of rap. (One kid has to be conservative in every family, it seems.) So I invited Robert's parents and naturally his mother went into psychic panic over the Zen Buddhist priest. 'A rabbi, even, or judge, please,' she begged.

Whose wedding was it anyway, my mother-in-law's, or the Zen Buddhist priest's, or our kids'? We cancelled. It seemed kind of perfect to have all the trappings and no wedding. The wedding happened the day we met and we were finally getting down to the party part.

Several years later we woke up one morning and decided to take a trip downtown to City Hall. We took the two kids who happened to be with us and did the thing. The lady of the couple in front of us had pink plastic curlers in her hair. So much for romance. Afterwards, we had *café lattés* at our favorite café and then Rob went to work. I guess that's why I can never remember the date. I always think of our anniversary as the day we met.

Getting married hasn't changed us much. Maybe if we weren't married he wouldn't have had the nerve to get a pair of blue lizard cowboy boots just like my black ones. I ordered a pair of custom boots and then heard my husband tell the salesgirl, 'I'll take a pair just like hers in blue.'

I thought, 'He must be kidding. We'll look like twins.' Have you ever tried to hide your feet? The other day I saw an elderly couple in Sacramento mall in identical T-shirts. He had his arm around her and they were lost in each other. I started thinking that maybe identical boots were just a beginning and began to imagine us in twin Armani suits riding the escalator at Bloomingdales or Harrods.

I do love this guy. The monogamy part was simple for me. I had blown puberty before we met and was really ready to fall into the same arms every night. Intimacy was the next step. I'm still discovering sex with my lover after 15 years. Maybe it's taken that long to reach the depth of my vulnerability, to find our rhythms, our body language, to enter the waves and cycles of motion and change in our relationship with trust and innocence.

Now, even though there are four sons and a cat in our family, only the cat lives at home. Robert massages him with slow hands, hands that are losing their grip. We are growing old together. I see my gray hair on his head, feel my muscles tighten in his body. We are mirrors of the best and worst in each other.

My ego lives in the past while Robert's roams the future. He projects himself into space and figures out all the variables, while I rehash and rearrange what's already gone down. Sometimes we get stuck in the same patterns – the angular, brittle movements, the icy silence all turned in on itself, the pretense it's not happening, the dark sighs and feigned willingness to hear each other out.

In other words, sometimes we're pathetic. Just last week, his victim was competing with mine for supremacy. We caught ourselves and laughed. That's the beauty of time and repetition. A long-term relationship has its waves, its cycles, its seasons, and they don't always match. Sometimes I'm hot, sometimes I'm not. Sometimes I need inner space and Robert needs social contact. I'm spending a week alone as I write this and I find that I'm filling my days much as I would with Robert. There's a rhythm to the way we are together and it's very similar to the way we are alone.

We've buried our fathers, put four kids through college and taken one through a marriage and divorce. We've owned two houses, said goodbye to at least four couches and three rugs. We've met each other's childhood friends and cruised the neighborhoods where we grew up. We've met a few of each other's ex-lovers and lived through it. And we've made a lot of music together.

The key to a relationship is all in the details. I married a guy who ruffles his hair and walks with his hands in his back pockets. He's a word man addicted to the New York Times Sunday crossword puzzle. I've never done one, nor do I expect I will. He's a punster, a word monster and a yenta who reads the tabloids. He's a carbo-man. Give him a meal of rice, potatoes, pasta, and beans. He talks in broken English to foreigners. I make fun of him and hear myself do the same thing.

I ponder decisions, Robert makes them on the beat and doesn't look back. I mull over the appropriateness of it all. I save things, he shreds them. I spend, he saves. When he finishes a meal he's ready to run. I enjoy lingering over tea and conversation. He wants to taxi home, I prefer walking. He arrives at airports an hour early, I get there just on time.

He breaks in my jeans, gives me the olive from his martinis, sends me flowers for no reason, edits my writing, massages the dreams trapped in my thighs and has more faith in me than I can muster for myself. I married a kind, loving man like my dad. I married a man who watches late-night TV and now I do the same. He smokes one cigarette in our blue bathtub at night. I wish I could. He eats bagels loaded with butter, cream cheese and poppy seeds. I hate poppy seeds and eat bran muffins plain.

He holds his breath when he talks on the phone, I remind him to breathe. He gets up and gets the Sunday Times and bagels. I make the coffee and turn on the classical station. He takes care of the cat. I watch over the plants. He tells people he has a green thumb but I've never seen it. He grew up in the same place and I grew up in several. I moved, he stayed still and we met anyway.

And during all of the above, he is part of me. I can't imagine any other. Isn't love strange?

ROBERT ANSELL

Thanks for your invitation to write about my relationship with Gabrielle. Frankly, it's not something I think about. Or worry about. Or work on, or process, or agonize over, or therapize. I think that's part of its beauty. My marriage just is. The *thought* of it occupies no portion of my daily consciousness, but the *experience* of it is the bedrock of my everyday reality. It's a psychic 'given'. It's just not something I think about.

Now that I'm thinking about it, it's hard to imagine that any of my thoughts would be of interest to anyone other than me. Or to me, for that matter, since it has taken me 14 years to 'think' about it.

I certainly don't have any answers to any questions anyone might have about relationship. I happen to be in one that has no real tension; it's a hum. And, I have no insights or rules that would help anyone else to achieve or maintain this equilibrium. For all I know, it could be as simple as the fact that, in Gabrielle's presence, I take on some of the more essential qualities of a cocker spaniel.

I'm sure our marriage has the potential for great conflict. We are both very strong, independent people. We spend a lot of time in creative projects, a burial ground for many relationships. We have spent long periods of time together, 24 hours per day, seven days per week. We have spent long periods of time apart. Each of these factors could be deadly. They haven't been. I don't know why.

We are, in many respects, psychic opposites. The basic movement of her mind is expansion; mine is contraction. Gabrielle likes to sail with ideas to their outer dimensions. I like to grab their four corners and reduce them to a neat knot. She is very open emotionally; I am not. She is creative; I am analytical. She shops; I don't. So, I don't have the faintest idea of what makes our marriage 'work'. Maybe it's because, as she once said, we are each other inside out. I don't know. When I look for a metaphor, it seems that she is my kite and I am her string.

I know I'm supposed to offer something meaningful to you, but it seems to me that marriages (or 'relationships') either work or they don't, and no amount of theorizing, analyzing or philosophizing can change those circumstances. I don't see how any thought, work or effort can create unity between two people. Chemistry; it's got to be about chemistry.

And trust. A relationship without trust is a treaty, not a marriage. And with trust comes vulnerability. My wife can hurt me. If she couldn't, she would not be my wife. I basically trust that she won't. Basically. Generally. On the whole. As a rule. Usually. Sure, I've suffered sexual jealousy, but never, ever for more than 16 or 17 hours a day. And there are always the day-to-day slings and arrows. But that all has more to do with the need to feed the 'victim' part of my ego than any reality, and has come to be more a part of my past than my present. I guess I just choose to spend less of my time there.

On my part, I have no struggle with monogamy. My commitment has nothing to do with formality or with any 'contract' that I have with Gabrielle. Maybe it's because I love her so dearly; maybe it's just a function of age. Either way, I have no real interest in physical intimacy with anyone else. And, if a passing interest should arise, I can always remember that I am married to a shaman. This is no energy to mess with. One spell cast and I could awaken one morning with my left testicle a distant memory.

Anyway, trust came for me immediately with love and deepened with time. And that allowed for surrender, the basic ingredient of our marriage. It's what Gabrielle teaches and something I've learned from her. In my work, I've moved from my context to hers; from a criminal law practise to the land of music, theater, production and business administration; from the place of 'Who's the lady with Robert?' to 'Who's the guy with Gabrielle?' Actually, from one side of my brain to the other.

I resisted her work at first. Maybe it was fear; maybe it was just because shamanism was so foreign to my experience. Eventually, I let go of all that. I even spent some time as her student, formally, in rooms full of her other students. Not a big deal, as it turned out. Once I surrendered, all I had to do was float with the river. It ran to the sea.

We surrender a lot to each other in our day-to-day lives. Our marriage is very much in balance in that way; it moves back and forth, be it our earning power or the roles we play of masculine/feminine, student/teacher, leader/follower. Except, of course, when it comes down to what video to rent tonight.

Anyhow, all this trust, surrender, balance – sounds kind of gooey, a little too ideal. It's not as though we don't have day-to-day problems, or 'situations', or tensions, whatever words we would put on those things that come between us. The thing is, they don't really come between us.

Obviously, Gabrielle has more to do with this than I do. Relating is not my long suit, by any means. It is Gabrielle's. And beyond that, she is, after all, a student and teacher of human nature who has a profound understanding of the ego/essence struggle. So, there aren't a lot of places for either of us to hide, she from herself or me from her. We just don't get trapped when our ego patterns collide with each other, or we don't get trapped for long. It's not easy to walk around for too long a time with your head sagging, shoulders slumped, eyes downcast, wrists limp and lower lip dangling when your partner won't play the game.

I know what you're thinking now. What a boring relationship. Well, I guess you're right. I really don't have anything to offer. It took us 11 years to get married. I don't know what that means. We make love when we both feel like it. I don't know what that means, either. It all just seems to hum along.

The only thing I do know is that I love my wife, deeply, and that underlying well continually feeds the spring. It's what makes all the rules, stratagems, theories and techniques of 'relationship' irrelevant. You've got the juice or you don't. I've got it. With her. To her. From her. She fills me up.

So, my friends, I hate to disappoint you and I really wish I had something helpful to contribute. I assure you it's not from lack of trying.

Jenner Roth & Terry Cooper

JENNER ROTH

Terry and I first met in January 1972 at a Group Relations Training Association conference at Southampton University, where I was one of the trainers. Before the conference started, we organized the composition of the groups, using the cards which each participant had filled in on application, giving their name, profession, sex, age, and so on. One name on those cards stood out: Terry Cooper. That was all – there was no 'Dr', 'Mr', 'Mrs', 'BA' or anything, simply 'Terry Cooper'. I did not even know whether Terry was a man or a woman, but I liked the simplicity; I felt that this was someone to whom I could relate, and I put Terry into my own group. It was not until we met that I realized he was a man – young, very attractive, with sort of golden hair, extremely warm and friendly, and easy in himself.

Over the week of the conference I was more and more impressed with Terry, with his honesty, his intensity, his passion, his fullness of who he was as a person, his ability to cry, his ability to be angry, his strength, his hardness, his softness. I think he was probably the fullest, richest person I had met, most unashamedly himself, even in his embarrassment about his high-heeled blue boots and his Afghan coat.

At one point during the workshop we acknowledged that we were attracted to each other, but agreed that we would not pursue a sexual relationship for a variety of reasons, among which were that I didn't feel it was appropriate to have a relationship with somebody I was working with, and that Terry was in love and engaged to be married. It felt very good to reach that decision and realize we would go on being friends and colleagues for a long time.

I was at a crossroads in my own career, thinking about whether I wanted to do more work in management and organization development or whether I wanted to work more with the therapeutic humanistic psychology approach. Terry proved to be the holding force for me in what I believed about honesty, straightforwardness, the possibility of change, that life could be better, that things could work out, and that there was a purpose in working on ourselves. As a result of knowing Terry, I made the choice to move more fully into humanistic therapy, away from management and business work and the more analytical, traditional way of looking at those things. It was a professional watershed for me.

Our relationship evolved over the next four years, as friends and colleagues. Terry's marriage ended in the autumn of 1975. In the winter of 1976, we decided that we wanted to be together and have a full and sexual relationship. It was a magical time and I realized that it would be my failure if this relationship did not work. I could not blame my partner this time; I could not make the excuse that he was not the right man, or that this or that was wrong with him. He had faults and difficulties, as we all do, but I knew that whatever might be wrong with Terry would not be what was wrong with our relationship. I knew that our communication was good, that he was very bright, that he was very full, that there wasn't anything missing. There was no way that I could ever blame that, and that was very important.

It was also very scary for me at that stage to change from the security of being his friend and colleague, with the enormous amount of respect and love for him that I had, to the risk of entering a sexual relationship with him. My sexual relationships had generally been less significant in my life than my professional relationships and friendships; I hadn't been good at maintaining or ending them well or staying good friends. My sexual relationships were the easiest to get into and the easiest to escape – in a sense they were important to me and intense, but in the longer term most awkward. I feel sad about this and

I think it was part of my own lack of clarity about sexuality at that time, some kind of shame that I still felt about being a sexual person.

We started living together in November 1976 and married in August 1978. Why did we make the statement of marriage? I think we each have separate stories about this, as we have about many things, including most of the movies we see! But Terry felt strongly that the commitment and effect of marriage were important, and that making a statement to the world and to ourselves did make a difference. I felt the opposite: that getting married would be an empty ritualization of our relationship. For me, the fact that we were *not* married kept my commitment to being there more alive. I recommitted myself every day; I was constantly questioning it, looking at it and making that extra effort.

In my first marriage I had resigned myself to how a marriage 'should' be and how a wife 'should' be. This was my view, not my husband's. I didn't speak up or take a position; I diminished myself; I felt I had to be very smiling, and I think I took a lot out of myself and out of that first marriage by those attitudes. I felt that *I* did not work in marriage and my fear was that I would be the same the second time around. I was so totally committed to Terry that I could not understand how anything would make a difference. In fact, I believed that the act of marriage, in itself, was bad for relationships.

Terry, however, was very clear that it was not the act of marriage that messed up relationships. Marriage was important to him: he wanted it a lot and kept talking about it. I was touched and moved that he wanted to commit himself and be with me; it meant an enormous amount to me and I felt that I could not fully accept this gift of his desire to be with me unless I could respond to it, knowing how much it meant to him. After a lot of listening and thinking, I decided, well, why not?

We shared our fantasies about getting married and, after a lot of discussion, we decided that we would elope. That was my need; I wanted to find out if I could stay myself while being married, and I felt that the way I could best do that would be to get married without telling anybody about it. I needed to find out whether my attitude was my own internal mythology or was pressure from the outside and, either way, whether I could deal with it.

We were married at 12 noon on Thursday 10 August. We walked to Camden Town Hall and had a moment's silence before the ceremony. It was lovely: I liked that we walked there, I liked that it was simple and I liked that we walked back. It was the antithesis of the pressures of most weddings, so I had already started well in this marriage.

However, by the time we reached the New Forest that evening for a few days of honeymoon, my entire body had come out in large boils and I could hardly move. Terry was marvellous; he took care of me, bathed me, put me to bed, and rushed off to Bournemouth to get ice-cream because that's all I could bear to eat. I felt so ill that we came home a day early and I went to the doctor.

My first thought was that everything in me was protesting – I should not have got married, it was the wrong thing to do. Gradually I realized that part of me knew it *had* been the right thing to do, but that I had not appreciated how much pain and anxiety remained from my first marriage. There was also the feeling that this marriage was for life, which was a complex and confusing realization. Somebody had said to me many years before, 'Jenner, you need a safe harbour,' and now, in some way, I suddenly felt really safe for the first time in my life – and that allowed everything to surface. It was as though all the toxins and fears came out in those boils.

We told my parents about the marriage early that autumn and they were wonderfully supportive. They had eloped, so there was a family history of eloping. They had also married somebody from another background, and Terry and I bring differences of culture, country, education, religion, age and class to our relationship. So we were continuing the history of mixed marriages that had lasted and worked within my family. I have often wondered how much of a script that was for me: that our marriage had a chance of working for what might seem to be all the wrong reasons, but within my family history were the right ones.

To my relief, I discovered that being married didn't change me, that it wasn't the fact of being married that had turned me into a submissive half-person. That was very important for me. I know that freedom has been the single most important motivating factor in my life, and there was a strong need in me to know that I could be free while being married with Terry. By not publicly acknowledging that I was married, which traditionally means belonging to somebody or becoming Mrs somebody, I was able to have my cake and eat it too and it was good. Freedom and love: I don't know how they fit together but they do.

Over the years, bit by bit, the importance of being married, of making that statement to each other, has grown in me and I am really glad that we did it. I'm glad that Terry took that stand. I think he was right.

It is difficult to say what difference marriage has made, except that it feels good and profound. Terry does not give his word easily or commit himself to things; his usual way is, 'Well, I'll see how I feel' (this includes whether we're going to go to a movie on Saturday night or moving to Timbuctoo), so I also appreciate increasingly what the commitment from him meant. Marriage bonds us in some way as a family that not being married didn't and I don't think would have. I can still choose to leave or choose to stay and there are many days when I deliberately have to make that choice to stay, but the fact of marriage has shifted, or freed and focused, what I do with the energy of choice. It is no longer a daily question of 'Am I going to leave or stay?' but has become 'How am I going to make this work for both of us? How am I going to keep the communication system open, how am I going to be honest?'

We have laughed sometimes about the fact that I had to come all the way from St Paul, Minnesota, through various other cultures, times, places and jobs, and reach Southampton University to run a one-week course in order to meet Terry Cooper; and how he had to go through all his past difficulties to become a group worker at that conference so that chance could bring us together. Then when we had our son, Jodie, we thought: aha, the whole purpose of it all had been not to get *us* together but to get us together to have *Jodie*, and there is a kind of delight and humour about that. What *is* our real purpose?

I think we stay together because we challenge each other, we care for each other, we are honest with each other. We share a passion for life, ideas, involvement, and a willingness to be stimulated and angered and delighted. We believe in the fact of spirituality, that it constantly and consistently manifests in the world and in people and everything around us. We believe that honesty and communication are not techniques but the basis for good relationships. We believe that within the family, within our larger family, within the community, within the world, things can be better. We believe that there is a difference between good and bad. We believe that basically we're OK and so is everybody else.

There are certain things that we do not share, but there is much more that we do. We are willing to share in each other's beliefs – Terry has been willing to take on things that I believe when he has understood or appreciated them, as I have been able to take on things that he believes. Underneath it all, underpinning it all, we both have enormous goodwill and we care for each other.

There is also the extra dimension of our work. We came to the same profession, one that is very important to us. Work has been a major commitment all our lives for each of us in different ways. I felt very excited about the possibility of having a relationship with a person who understood my commitment to my work, and also understood exactly what my work was and could appreciate the complexities of it. I knew sometimes in the past my partner in a personal relationship has been jealous of therapeutic relationships in my work and has felt left out. That has never been the case with Terry.

Over the past 18 years Terry and I have benefited not only from working together but also from working jointly with other couples, in individual private work and in groups. Most of us are isolated in our relationships and the closest we come to public information is what we see on television or on the street or what we experienced in our family homes. Usually those models don't help us very much and so we feel alone as a couple dealing with intimacy and other issues. A number of years ago we started running an annual workshop for couples who actively want good relationships and who are working towards them, struggling day to day with little difficulties and larger ones, and this has also been very supportive of Terry and me as a couple.

In 1988 we began to teach PAIRS (Practical Application of Intimate Relationship Skills), a psycho-educational programme which is clearly and specifically about learning the skills that can facilitate a good relationship. Its premise, with which we agree whole-heartedly, is that the most essential features of a good relationship are goodwill and good communications. If those two are alive and well, then you can work through just about anything.

So working with other couples' relationships is another thing that we share.

I see myself as committed to this relationship with Terry for life. He is the most important person in my life, along with our son Jodie – each goes foreground and background at different times for me. I still feel, as I felt at the beginning, that Terry is a good person for me to be with and that the difficulties are things that we can and should work out.

A major part of my commitment is monogamy. To what degree? 100 per cent, 200 per cent, 300 per cent – totally, completely – that's the degree. 360 degrees. How do I say 'fully'? I feel that monogamy, committing myself to somebody sexually, is absolutely essential. That might seem ironic after what I said about the ease with which I entered and left previous sexual relationships, but I think my attitude changed a lot when I realized that to open myself up to somebody sexually was a very profound experience.

I feel that I have a healthy attitude towards sex: I like it with the person I love, I'm not easily bored by it, I'm very catholic in my tastes. Having sex with somebody that I really love and respect makes it very intimate – it is a way in which I can share myself and be vulnerable without feeling threatened. There's something that happens for me in a committed sexual relationship that makes it untenable if my partner is having a sexual relationship with anybody else. I've looked at it a lot at various times and in various ways and have realized that it is just too painful to open myself up to somebody sexually and have them taking that energy, space and commitment elsewhere. It feels like a profound betrayal and I am not prepared to accept it. For me, it is grounds for the end of a relationship – I will not have a relationship with a person unless it is monogamous. For me it would be some kind of lie, something that isn't being dealt with or talked about or shared between the two of us. I don't feel that socially, I don't feel it intellectually, but I do feel it sexually and in terms of loyalty and commitment.

What I have seen and experienced is that when a relationship is not monogamous there is a constant holding back in the relationship. That works for some people, but it doesn't work for me. I need monogamy: it is absolutely the bottom line for me.

Sexuality plays a very important part in my relationship – I would not want to live without sex. Terry is a very good sex partner; he is healthy, giving and thoughtful, and sex is important to him. He keeps it alive for us in many more ways than I do (though there are other things I keep alive). It is very important to me that Terry is a sexual person, that he likes sex, that he feels good about sex, that he wants to have sex. It isn't *the* most important thing, but I wouldn't want to have a relationship without it. It brings us together when we've been apart, it allows us to connect when we don't have any other way of connecting, it allows us to put the final stamp on something that's been good or exciting, and it often relieves tension or anxiety for one or the other of us. So it plays a very full part.

Do I ever feel any conflict between my individual sense of purpose and my sense of identity within our relationship? Yes and no. For me, learning to live in an intimate relationship and maintain a sense of my own self, of who I am and what I believe in, is the single most difficult lesson in my life. I still have to work on my old patterns and messages in the struggle to maintain my sense of self, though I'm improving and am increasingly able to be fully myself within my family and particularly in my relationship with Terry, which is where I was most inhibited. There was a time when, if Terry did not like something, I felt that I had to change it, but now I look carefully at whether change is necessary or whether he and I can live with the dislike. My immediate response is no longer 'Oh lord, I've done the wrong thing – I must be wrong.' That has been an enormous step for me and it feels good and healthy for both of us. It is no longer a case of either going under or leaving my partner, as it was so often in earlier relationships.

Terry and I are partners in a business, we share friends and colleagues, we have the same purpose, the same belief system. We do, however, have different ways of going about what we do, both in our individual and group work and in developing and managing Spectrum, a centre for humanistic psychology, which sometimes puts us in conflict, particularly if we don't understand each other. Terry is more pro-active and will go all out for something, whereas my tendency is to maintain, to be in the background, to watch from behind, to wait, to organize, and those contrasts sometimes leave us open to misunderstandings or conflict.

In little everyday things, conflict can arise when Terry does something I don't like, and that depends on what day of the week it is or in what kind of mood I woke up! On some days I don't like it if he doesn't say hello right, or doesn't hang his coat up. Terry lets go of things but my tendency is to hold on to them. There is actually more anger than conflict in our relationship – flare-ups about specific things or moments. Terry is much quicker to express his irritation or dislike of something than I am. I am quicker to apologize, but if I confront Terry because he has been angry and has not understood, or he recognizes that he was out of line, I appreciate enormously that he will go away and think about things; he will admit that he was wrong and say that he is sorry.

Conflict comes for us out of tiredness, stress, lack of communication. There are very few issues for conflict if we have the time and space to talk about them, deal with them, understand each other. If we are both very tired and Terry comes home and I haven't fixed dinner, then he may be angry; or if he's fixed dinner and I haven't told him I would be late, he feels angry and there will be conflict. Sometimes there is conflict about one of us wanting time: perhaps Terry has come home and had dinner and watched some TV, I've put Jodie to bed that particular night, and Terry wants some time with me and I'm too tired and he'll be irritable. If one of us isn't taking care of ourselves and is getting ill or dragging on the energy, we tend to get irritated by that. (I think it's also that we don't like seeing the other person tired or not feeling well and it's painful for us.)

What is it that makes our relationship alive? I think it is 'living' rather than 'alive', though there are moments when it feels alive and growing and vibrant. A lot of our time is spent dealing with life's issues: personal problems that any of the three of us may have, education problems, taking the cars to the garage or the letters to the post office, doing the laundry, walking the dogs. We function; we go along, we go along, we go along. There is a lot of love, a lot of taking care of each other, supporting each other, and we have little moments of being 'alive'. I think sex keeps our life alive, and the fact that we are both intelligent and bright and curious. And friendliness – all three of us enjoy people and like talking to them and being with them, and other people being around us helps to keep the relationship alive. Continuing to share with each other who we are and what's going on in our lives also keeps our relationship alive.

And love? My experience of love is safety, warmth, excitement, affection, being met, being responded to, being cared for and about, having nice things done. My understanding of love is different from my understanding of being *in* love. Love, for me, encompasses affection and hatred and anger and need and a lot of things. It means caring for each other, doing that bit extra for each other, thoughtfulness – lots of little thoughtful things, like telephone calls, saying hello and goodbye, kissing each other when we come home or leave, making contact, constantly trying to say who I am for the other person, letting him know what's happening, making the effort, making the relationship a priority, caring about what the other person wants and needs.

Love is something that is constant, whatever else goes on, and knowing that this is the person that I want to be with. It is the underlying melody that is always there, that makes me know that this is right for me. No matter what other tunes may be played, there's this single melody that goes through. Sometimes, if I'm very cut off from myself or very angry with Terry, or if he is angry with me, that melody goes background and it's difficult to hear; but when I listen, it is there, and that is love. It goes on and I know – it's a felt knowledge – that I *do* love Terry and that I *do* have goodwill towards him and that this *is* who I want to be with. And it makes me keep trying, it makes me put out more energy when I feel fed up or tired or sick of trying. It makes me determined to talk about it, to tell him how I feel, to apologize, to confront him, to respond, to do that bit extra – whatever it is that I feel is demanded. And I feel that I get that back as well.

There is a spiritual dimension, too, in the manifestation of love and goodwill towards others, a sense of awe in the world, in the birth of our child, in the dutifulness of our dogs, in our garden, our home, each other, the sun, people's kindness and goodwill, pleasure, warmth. There are ritual moments in our family life and personal life, and a very deep sense of connection with our higher selves.

TERRY COOPER

I am now in my second marriage. My wife, Jenner, and I are both psychotherapists and we have an 11-year-old son, Jodie. In my relationship with Jenner there are basically four areas that really make it work for me: I feel loved; there is constant communication; I feel respected as an emotional, thinking, physical person; and I am constantly affirmed and stroked and made to feel good about myself. All of these qualities of feeling I reciprocate and a lot of my time is spent maintaining those aspects of the relationship. To maintain respect, love and communication takes a tremendous amount of time, energy and goodwill, but no intimate relationship can survive unless a couple is prepared to put that time and those attitudes into practice.

That doesn't mean that I feel wholly fulfilled in my relationship with Jenner. I don't. There are differences – in the way that we would choose to use our free time, in our ways of responding to situations and dealing with them, and even in how we feel in situations. But really those differences are not what makes the relationship difficult; they are not even accountable for the unfulfilled parts of the relationship, which are about me, my relationship to myself, how I bring my history, my luggage, my attitudes and expectations from what I perceived in my own family was the way to have a relationship. My English working-class background and history gave me a different kind of psychology to Jenner, who was from a middle-class American background, and we have needed to understand our own histories in order to understand some of the conflicts, particularly our conflicting expectations around parenting. Most of my lack of fulfilment in the relationship is based on my own unresolved issues, from my own growing up and my own background.

It is important to look at what each person is bringing into a relationship from their past – not only universal cultural expectations but also the individual history, the individual background that we bring in, the different picture we have of what a relationship is going to be. Many of us look at a relationship initially for what we can get out of it and we don't really consider what we are taking into it.

In order to be close and intimate, in order to have a relationship that grows, we do have to give up things we have learned, established beliefs, attitudes that we rely on. We have to shed some skins in order to continue growing. In a sense the 'me' that I am developing in my marriage now is a new me; it is a blend of some of the attitudes and feelings and thoughts from my past with some of the new ones that I am learning in my current relationship, and also the different learnings that come from having a child and becoming three – forming a family with no history. A child contributes altogether different ingredients to a relationship, and beginning to form a family changes a lot of things. Children bring information in from God knows where and a child coming into a relationship feeds and nourishes and offers very important information to the parents.

Looking back, I am now pretty sure that I married my first wife in an attempt to make the relationship work and to take another step in the hope of making it more meaningful on some level. I did not marry for any religious or moral reasons; I married because it was a ritual to go through that might somehow magically improve the quality of my life.

It had been a very public wedding, involving all sorts of people. But when I married Jenner, we both wanted to keep it private and low-key, with a few friends as witnesses simply to cover the legal aspects. I think that the decision to marry was based more on my feelings than on hers; I don't think Jenner really needed to get married, but I needed to go through a ritual that made me feel more secure. Jenner had more experience then of being alone, not in a relationship; she had also experienced long-term relationships and I think that she was more confident than me. I felt that marriage would help me feel more confident and would add balance to our relationship. And it did; it was another kind of affirmation, from her to me, and the ritual gave me indirect reassurance (I'm not easy to reassure directly). It was a symbolic communication that went quite deep between us.

From the beginning our relationship was based on monogamy. It was explicit between us that if we messed around with anybody else, that would be it – the relationship would not continue. One of the factors that has helped me discipline myself in our contract is my respect for Jenner's word, because I believe that really would be her position. At first the contract worked equally well for me: I didn't want to have other relationships and I certainly didn't want her to. Later, however, I went through a phase of feeling that it would not be the end of the world for me if she did have an affair and I felt somehow that this fantasy showed how secure I was feeling in the relationship. Whether in reality I would have felt the same way if she actually had had an affair, I very much doubt! I think there would have been a lot of upset and problems.

One of my envies is that Jenner shows more satisfaction with the relationship than I do. But then she also appears to be more content in other areas of her life than I am. She tends to accept situations, whereas I tend to believe that the grass is greener on the other side. I have a compulsive kind of adventurer in me. At heart I am a kid who loves to play and find out and explore and sometimes tries to make things different for the sake of making them different. In my earlier days, that behaviour was very destructive: I became a drug addict and eventually sought treatment in a therapeutic community, which is what brought me into therapy 22 years ago.

So my impulse control is not as strong as Jenner's. That is not to say that I have fucked around, because I have not. The relationship has always meant too much to me for me to do that, though I have wanted to and I have become obsessed a couple of times with different women. The way that I dealt with that was to whine to Jenner – I can only describe it as a kind of whine – pleading with her to let me off the hook so that I could have a sexual relationship.

I have never, ever wanted to leave Jenner since we started an intimate relationship 16 years ago, and so the pain of sharing my feelings with her about other women, the pain of opening myself up to the possibility of another short-term relationship, and looking at the effect of that on Jenner and the kind of pressures that puts her under, just isn't worth it to me. A part of me thinks that I could do that and not feel guilty, but the reality is that I have felt guilty whenever I've become emotionally involved with somebody else, and I do not feel comfortable about that.

Monogamy, then, has not always been easy for me but, as a therapist, I have noticed over the years how many relationships have been bruised and shattered by affairs, even in so-called open relationships. Many years ago some friends of mine had an open relationship and seemed to handle it well for a number of years, until suddenly one of them wanted to marry somebody else and that was the end of that. I have yet to see any open marriages or relationships working really successfully in the long term and this has reinforced for me the importance of maintaining my own monogamous contract with Jenner.

It has helped that the contract itself is explicit. It was something that we both agreed upon and talked about so that there was no ambiguity – and I know only too well that the impulsive part of me looks for ambiguity when it wants what it wants. Jenner has always been quite clear about her boundaries; she is specific and open about the consequences of what is important to her and, in a way, I have used that defined, grounded, solid part of her a lot in our relationship to balance out my impulsiveness. In many ways I have learned discipline through Jenner and that has been good for me because my life was so chaotic and unbounded for many years. For me, then, to have a structure and a clearly defined relationship comes as a great freedom, though I can understand that that is not true for everybody. Jenner sometimes tends to become fixed and rigid and she says that I am good for her in that I challenge those parts of her.

This difference in attitude between us was crystallized when we were working in Brazil in 1978 and went to see a Condomblé priestess. As soon as we entered her room, the priestess threw some shells down onto the table and read them. She made a very simple and clear statement that absolutely summed up our relationship. She looked at Jenner and said, 'You hold on to things too much and you need to learn how to let them go.' Then she looked at me and said, 'And you let go of things too much and you need to learn how to hold on to them.' That observation was true and profound – it went right to the bones of our relationship and over the years we have used the knowledge of it. Jenner has been as patient about me learning to discipline my impulsiveness as I have been patient with her learning to be more flexible and to let go some more.

We seem to be two halves of a piece that belong together. We balance one another. I tend to be a more emotional person, she tends to be more rational; I am impulsive, she is more grounded; and we each bring our own qualities and characters as our contribution to the relationship. People are consistent and I think we shall probably both be dealing with this polarization of groundedness and impulsiveness in ourselves and in our relationship for the rest of our lives. No doubt we shall refine these issues; we have become less charged about them, more accepting, and when they represent conflicts we get through them a lot more quickly now than before.

I see our relationship continuing into old age and I look forward to spending more and more time together. I try to see us in the long term as healthy, aging people, but at the same time I try to look at it bifocally and live one day at a time and do the best I can each day. After 13 years of marriage it sometimes amazes me as I drive home from work when I realize that I am still excited about going home and seeing Jenner. I had some fears, left over from my first marriage, that four years was as long as it could last, but I've more than trebled that time now and I definitely feel that this is still where I want to be. And that feels incredibly satisfying. The obsessions I had about other women have made me even more committed to Jenner and I just hope that we continue to be healthy so that we can manifest that long-term vision and share that time together.

One of the factors that has helped us transcend any differences is that we are both givers. We care a lot for one another and we both *give*, so that there is plenty to go around. I would hate to be a taker and to be in a relationship with someone who was a taker! We are both givers, expecting to put a lot more into the relationship than we take out – and that feels right to me, that feels good. We are also generous people, so that issues about money have never really been a problem; we share whatever we have. It all just goes into the pot like everything else and is there to be taken out and used. Generosity is a very important part of our relationship and that's certainly true sexually as well: we are both very generous and very loving and caring with one another sexually – we want to please one another so we both end up feeling pleased!

Sex is a vital part of my relationship with Jenner. If sex wasn't good, I could be talking about a whole different relationship, and I'm not even sure that there would be a relationship at all without it. I am a very sexual person and I cannot imagine being unable to share my love sexually to express the depth of our relationship – I need to be able to *live* with someone in that sense. I enjoy sex so much with Jenner that it is hard to imagine what would happen without it. Sexuality is an important kind of communication for me.

Communication was one of the four important areas I mentioned earlier, and one of the keys in dealing with sex, money and other issues is talking about them. Two people who care about one another and love one another can deal with most events and tragedies in the life of the relationship as long as they can sit down and talk in a caring, concerned way, especially if they share the expectation that discussion can resolve many of the issues or at the very least make them feel better about dealing with them.

In the area of sexuality it is particularly important to be explicit about what you want and what you don't want. An old teacher of mine, Stanley Keleman, once said, 'Loving someone is the willingness to educate them about who you are,' and I think that is a wonderful definition of love and a very necessary part of making a relationship succeed. That saying summarizes the feelings of love and is a recognition of what the relationship needs. One of the ways that we can establish a balance of power in a relationship is to empower our partner by giving them information about ourselves, about what we are going through and what we are feeling. For me, communication is essential and it needs to be explicit.

Another of the points I mentioned earlier which keeps my relationship with Jenner alive is respect for each other. This is crucial. For me, it means that Jenner is a complete person; she is able to express herself and be direct about what she wants, as I am. It means there is a balance of power within the relationship, which makes it dynamic and interesting for me. It means that both of us are willing to relate at the same level, intellectually, emotionally and physically, and our basic intention is to be in an 'I'm OK, you're OK' situation rather than seeking to be on top, metaphorically speaking, or on the bottom. So many relationships have diagonal rather than level power structures in which one person plays bottom dog and the other person plays top dog, so that the relationship is based on a power-and-submission game. Such relationships often lose their vitality because there is a confluence, a mutual agreement for one to be up and one to be down. Confluence is one of the major factors involved in reducing the amount of feeling and contact there is between two people.

One of the manifestations of such an imbalance might be that one partner is more skilled at expressing anger than the other. If one person is able to express anger and the other just stays hurt, then it is not an equal relationship: the power dynamics are in one person's favour. In that context, the person who is hurt and having anger expressed at them may need to learn how to communicate their own anger and not just turn it into tears. They need to assert themselves and meet the anger coming from the other person.

In my own relationship I became aware that there was a power imbalance and that it was based on the fact that Jenner and I come from very different worlds. My background was very violent and angry, hers was very middle-class and rational. This meant that I was able to express my anger a lot more readily and naturally. Jenner was also inhibited partly by the cultural conditioning that it is more acceptable for a woman to cry than to get angry. For some years Jenner would get hurt and I would get angry when we had a row, and I realized that it wasn't a fair fight. I could be a nastier person than she, I could say more hurtful things in a more aggressive way than was in her psychological make-up. Gradually I learned, through watching the effect of my anger on her, that if I could be nastier and assume a stronger and more dominant position, then in a way I had a greater responsibility to do something about that.

I realized that I had a weapon I could use, but must discipline myself not to use it. I had to find other ways of talking about the way I felt. She has learned over the years to become more comfortable about expressing her own anger and coming back at me when I have been angry. And that has been an important change in our relationship. I think that if I had continued to bully and stay on top in our conflicts, I would probably not be in the relationship now.

One of my goals in our relationship has been to reduce my angry response to situations, which used to limit me as if I was a one-stringed violin. When we had our son, Jodie, our life was very demanding, there was a lot of stress, and I would react angrily to any situation. I was awful to drive around with, for example, because whenever another driver put me in an awkward situation I would get furious, winding down the window and shouting until the veins stuck out on my neck. Jenner's response was always, 'Why do you get so angry?', which I took to mean, 'You shouldn't get angry.' And my response was to get angry with her instead and say, 'Well, you could see he pulled out in front of me – why don't you get angry at *him* instead of *me*?' And so it went on, her super-rational response and my super-angry one, and I always felt when she made that intervention that she was more concerned about the other person than about me. So I had no motivation to change; I just used to defend my feelings of anger and say, 'It's good to get anger out, and it's good to be expressive.'

Then one day she changed her response. She said, 'Oh, why do you get so angry? I just see what it does to you.' And I got curious because it sounded like there was some element of concern for me in it and I didn't understand what she was concerned about; after all, I was getting my anger out. She said, 'You know, I see that just after you have been through one of these bursts of anger you look so grey and exhausted.' And I thought, God, yes, that's exactly how I feel after those situations. I began to realize then that if you are attached to anger it becomes a defence, as every emotion can become a defence: sadness and hurt can become a defence against contact – all emotions can – but anger can be a particularly strong barrier. I realized that I had to acquire a different vocabulary; I had to learn how I was letting my levels of stress and anxiety (which were not words I applied to myself at the time) build up preceding these outbursts. I had to learn to control myself and my difficulties without exploding.

And I have succeeded in that. I am less angry now and much more appropriate with my anger in my family. It's not a pattern that I depend on to protect myself. It feels really good to recognize that I am not as angry as I used to be, and it feels as if my body is changing. Being angry as a pattern, as a lifestyle, was like working on a pneumatic drill every day – and what does that do to your body? A little bit of withholding is a good thing for me.

The differences between my impulsive, expressive behaviour and Jenner's controlling style have actually helped the relationship last for so long and have something to do with why I see it continuing into the future. It is based on there being very different parts of ourselves that we need to develop. I have learned from her to love, to be more rational and more understanding, therefore more disciplined and controlled in a positive way, and I think she has learned from me to be more expressive and responsive to needs. So we both have adequacies and inadequacies that we bring to the relationship, and one of the nice things about a long-term partnership is that those differences become blended, with both people putting different aspects, elements or ingredients of themselves into a pot sos that it is in there for everybody. A way of sharing power is to *recognize* that different people bring different things to a relationship, different energies and different emotional tones.

I think that I'm probably going to be working on and shaping and changing this part of me for the rest of my life, to find balance. And our such different styles, bound up with our deep affection and love for each other, is a combination that allows me to think of the relationship in the long term. We are constantly learning from one another and constantly challenging one another in a very positive kind of way.

We are full of curiosity. I think that is why we are therapists: there is a part of us that likes to play detective, and that curiosity motivates us to learn from each other. I don't know what it would be like to be with somebody I didn't feel I had anything to learn from – I don't think that's an equal relationship. I think that part of the balance of power lies in recognizing that you have something to learn from your partner, and usually it's something major that conflicts with your own upbringing and the messages and scripts that you developed during your growing up.

For me, the fact that we constantly communicate and interact around the ingredients each of us contributes to the relationship brings a spiritual dimension into it. The different parts of ourselves are like wall-bricks in a house, but the cement or spiritual quality that weaves itself through the relationship is us *communicating* about all of this, sharing and being open. One of the pictures I have of a healthy relationship is two people standing firm and being open, being as much on the ground as in the air, so that our personalities become a channel to let good energy and love through. If these so-called differences, or what people sometimes call obstacles in relationships, are not talked about, then there is a block to the flow of love and concern and care that the relationship could otherwise tap.

Relationships go through different phases – spiritual, psychological and practical. Sometimes Jenner and I are business partners working alongside one another, running Spectrum, shopping for food, picking Jodie up from school, organizing the baby-sitters and the central-heating boiler man, and life just has a practical dimension. Sometimes the relationship goes through a psychological phase where there's not a particularly high feeling and we are not particularly practically orientated, but we are concerned about and involved with one another on an emotional level, interested in how each other feels, what's going on in one another's life and whether we are happy with it. And sometimes we are on a high and feeling good, not necessarily high in terms of energy but moving up out of the psychological; we feel bonded but there's not a lot of talk – there is often quietness and reflection, and those times are really enjoyabie. And sometimes all of those exist, or a combination of two of them exists – it varies.

My relationship is the basis of my life; it is what gives everything else meaning and value.

Riane Eisler & David Loye

RIANE EISLER

It is a few days after David's birthday, his 66th and the 14th year that we have celebrated this occasion together. For me, it is indeed an occasion for celebration, a time to express my gratitude for the gift of our partnership and our love.

David and I met when I was in my middle forties. I had been married once before, and after my divorce raised two daughters, worked as an attorney, lecturer, organizer, researcher, and writer, and, above all, began to develop my own individual sense of purpose and destiny. One result was that I was increasingly ill-equipped to play the conventional supportive role that in what I call a dominator model of society is generally assigned to women. Yes, I certainly wanted to give of myself and of my love, to help my partner (as well as others). But I was no longer willing to do this at the expense of my own human development.

I thought sometimes that I had truly painted myself into a corner, as I found it increasingly impossible to date men who expected me to massage their egos, dance attendance upon them, and generally only reflect their interests and goals, as if I were a mirror. And then along came David.

It was a truly romantic beginning. We met, had lunch together, could not bear to part, finally said goodbye at 4 p.m. (because I had a business appointment), and met again for dinner that evening. Later that night, David stopped by my house again, to drop into my mailbox a poem. It was the first of many poems, which he continued to write to me, even though we now saw each other every single day. I in turn wrote him letters, trying to express my feelings, both my happiness and my concerns. Because when David met me I was quite ill, and I was afraid that if he found out he would leave me. But of course nothing of the sort happened, and instead he was a major, indeed critical, force in my healing.

Now our relationship is entering its 15th year. We did not marry right away. The reason was my fear of the roles of husband and wife, of the luggage of thousands of years when those roles were defined in terms of precisely the kind of relationship that I could not and did not want to adjust to. And I was so afraid that unconsciously we would both slip into those roles, as every one of us (particularly the women and men of our generation) has internalized these patterns. I think it was good that we did not marry right away, that we waited for a number of years to do so. For by then our relationship had become a true partnership, unencumbered by that dominator social script.

When we did marry, it was for a rather unorthodox reason. A man came to visit us one day who had lived with a woman for many years and she had died. He grieved terribly for her death, but also expressed a sense of bewilderment and even further grief that his loss was not generally recognized, because they had not been officially married. I by then was doing a lot of travelling, and I began to worry about what would happen should I suddenly die, not only because of the man's visit and what it had revealed about still prevailing prejudices, but also because I really wanted to be sure that the bonding between David and me would also carry over into a lifelong bonding between him and my daughters, for that continuity of family was so very important to me.

Still, we struggled (or at least I struggled) with this question of marriage. We had made our own contract, dealing with matters such as property, income, mutual responsibilities, etc. This was because in my work as an attorney I did some pioneering work on what I called at the time non-sexist marriage and non-marital contracts – what I would today call partnership contracts And I adapted one of these contracts that

I had written for a couple that I particularly liked, and with whom I identified in many ways, to our own needs. So technically there was really no need for us to marry. And yet the more we talked about it, somehow the ritual or symbol of marriage became important to us.

When we did marry, we had our own very special ritual. We chose to marry us a woman who was a minister of a small congregation and the marriage took place at her home. It was just the three of us. We cut fresh flowers from our garden. She wore beautiful colorful robes. David read some of his poetry to me. I read him my own special vows.

As I look back on it, it seems to me a very good way of doing things, getting married after you have lived together and already established your relationship for some time. Because our vows were very real, they were based on experience and on knowledge and on the deep and by then clearly committed and unconditional bond of our love.

We are very fortunate. I think the key word is compatibility. But it is not only a compatibility of enjoying so many of the same things – from sunsets and trees to humor and music (and we happen to love the same kind of music) and conversation. We share so many common beliefs and assumptions about life and love, about human possibilities for creativity and goodness, about the realistic possibility of reconstructing our values and institutions in a more pro-human direction. And, above all, we share the commitment to make those beliefs be of use to our community and to our world.

We also share a commitment to make our relationship work and to avoid dominator-dominated roles and tactics. And part of this commitment is to flexible roles, rather than rigid ones, so that we can truly be partners in a relationship that makes it possible for both of us to develop and grow. In that respect, David's commitment to our relationship has been a commitment also to my work. I do not think I could have done it without him, as I wrote in the introduction to my book, *The*

Chalice and The Blade. His belief in me, his belief in the importance of what I was doing and continue to do, his encyclopaedic knowledge about social science, and above all his willingness to give so generously of himself and his time have been invaluable. Indeed it is almost like a dream come true, to have someone who really does validate the best in me.

Sometimes when I speak about our relationship in the context of the partnership rather than dominator model, I speak about how under the old model only men are seen as being creative (with the only creative act that women are supposedly capable of being that magnificent act of giving birth – and even that is in creation stories usurped by a male deity). But in our relationship we are both creative. We are also both each other's muse – a very different situation from the conventional view that the muses are women and the men are creators. This is not to say that our relationship is solely intellectual. Touching, holding one another, sexuality, the bonding of pleasure is of course also very important to us.

Certainly we have problems and conflicts. I think it is unrealistic to expect a conflict-free relationship, particularly with someone that you see every day. In this respect we are fortunate that we each have our own workspaces: David in a large outside studio, and I in a smaller inside studio so that often I have books and folders all over the house. But I tend to be neater than David – and, in fact, this has been a source of some major conflicts, as I need, far more than he, an aesthetic and ordered space around me, and become unsettled if there is too much clutter, which David seems to produce with uncanny regularity.

We have also had in our time together periods of real crisis, times when misunderstandings and hurts seem to pile up and neither one of us could, or would, back off. But our conflicts, even though sometimes very painful, somehow manage to find resolution. Or rather, we both work very hard at finding ways of dealing with them – not necessarily finally and forever to resolve them, but to find that we can both feel more comfortable and respected at the same time that we do not necessarily agree or feel the same. We have developed a number of ways of doing that, none of them perfect, but still helpful.

One way, which I adapted from a technique called re-evaluation co-counseling, is that rather than dumping our feelings on each other (which we occasionally, of course, also do), we ask for a session when we are distressed. The basis of this session is that our distress usually is also rooted in earlier experiences, even though the other person may have done something that is upsetting in its own right. It is further based on the idea that we can take turns listening to each other, and on trying to do so without interrupting.

So what we do is to frame this session in positive terms, in validation for ourselves and for each other – a wonderful way of reminding ourselves that even though we may feel very angry or hurt at the moment, there are things about the other person that we truly cherish and admire. The session is framed as follows: the person who has asked for the session gets to speak and the other person gets to be the 'co-counselor', a role that requires taking a somewhat validating and 'healing' stance.

The session opens by the person who is taking the session saying what is new and good. This can be anything from a small item, like a special breakfast, to some recent good fortune. And, since it's hard to remember, what's new and good is that one had the good sense to ask for a session. The next thing is to say something that one likes about oneself. And the third thing is saying something one likes about the other person (which feels weird when one is furious at someone, but, as I said, does make it possible to see things in larger perspective). Next in the session is talking about the distress, including one's feelings as a reaction to what the other person did or said. Usually what happens is that earlier stuff also comes up. And it does act as something of a release. Finally, the session closes with the person taking the session talking about something that she or he is looking forward to.

I think tools are important in relationships, just as they are in all other areas of our lives. So this 'session' has been useful to us. But I think the main reason that such tools are useful to us is that we are willing to use them, and when necessary to try to fashion new ones. And basically the reason that we are willing, even though we both have a great many demands on our time, to devote time and energy to the fashioning and using of tools to maintain and strengthen our relationship is that we truly do value and love each other.

When I think of our love, it is not something separate from our friendship, from our intellectual partnership, and the fact that we like to take walks together by the sea, or that we rarely tire of each other's company. In other words, it isn't the conventional picture of romantic love. Nor is it by any means the conventional picture of domestic love, for we interchange roles that are stereotypically labeled masculine and feminine (and I will say more about that in a moment).

Rather, it is a more complete kind of love, based on friendship and companionship as well as sexual attraction, and yes, also what for us is a very strong spiritual bond. It is a bond of common ideals, of common perceptions (including a great deal of empathy for others in this world), and perhaps above all a shared faith that our lives, our work, and the great gift of having found one another, has some larger meaning, and that we were brought together in order to strengthen and nurture and support each other in a larger endeavor, our endeavor to make a contribution that can be of use, of healing, at this critical time in the history of our planet.

Ours is very much a spirituality of service, and it certainly is an immanent as well as a transcendent spirituality. It is in many ways much closer to that of the prehistoric peoples that I write about in *The Chalice and The Blade* and that we have both become so fascinated by, who managed to create social structures that were based more on power as symbolized by the chalice than by the blade.

All of which leads me back to a very basic matter that undergirds our relationship. This is the knowledge that while we have all as women and men been taught that the 'war of the sexes' is inevitable, there is another possibility: one where our linking rather than ranking is primary and in which both women and men can be both caring and nurturing and forceful and assertive. It is truly basic, because it makes it possible for us to recognize that to build a relationship that works for both of us requires that we continually try to free ourselves from the stereotypical gender roles in which men are supposed to 'wear the pants', or dominate, and women are supposed to submit and serve – and manipulate and placate, rather than directly assert their needs.

I think it is this recognition on *both* our parts that more than any other single thing makes David's and my relationship so much less tense and infinitely more satisfying than our earlier marriages.

It is late, as I finish writing this, and I realize that with the press of so many things we have not taken enough time to simply look back on our relationship, and to savor again what we have shared. For a while we tried to keep a journal, which we would write together at bedtime towards the end of the year, trying to summarize some of the highlights. But it has been years since we have taken the time to do that.

As I write this, I realize that it would be good to start doing our journal again, even though, as I too now approach 60, I find myself far more conscious of how I spend my time (which I always thought infinite). For even though there are books that I want to give most of my time to writing (as David does to writing his), perhaps this is something that we can also do as a kind of end-of-year ritual of reflection and thanksgiving for what we had both for so long despaired of finding: the wonderful years that have been given us to be together.

DAVID LOYE

Before I met Riane, I was leading a bewildered and lonely existence knocking like a pinball around the cold psychic corridors of Los Angeles. It always looks so great on the surface there, so sunny. But there are few places I know of where you can feel so lonely.

I had gone through a number of dead-end affairs and one day the woman who was typing the manuscript of my book *The Leadership Passion* said to me that she knew a wonderful woman I should meet and proceeded to describe her. She said this wonderful woman was in her early to mid-forties. That sounded about right. She was very good-looking, very bright, interested in the future. That sounded really great. She said this woman was interested in art and classical music and I thought to myself, This is too good to be true!

Then she said this woman was a lawyer and I began to tighten up just a little. She said, 'She's writing a book on divorce,' and the image began to harden. Then she said, 'Her name is Riane Eisler.'

Well, at that I really backed off rapidly inside because, for some crazy reason, this hard-edged name Eisler sounded to me like Eichmann, the killer of the Jews. Instantly there formed within me the image of a hard, cold character, tough as nails. So what I said on the surface was, 'Oh yeah, she sounds interesting,' but underneath I swore I would never go near that one.

For an entire year every so often this woman would bring her up. She would see me come crawling in from some unhappy affair and she would suggest this Riane Eisler once again and I would always say, 'Oh yeah, yeah, I'll have to look into that.'

Always, of course, reaffirming to myself, 'No sirree.'

Then one day I was sitting in my research office in Westwood Village – I was on the UCLA School of Medicine faculty at the time – and the phone rang and I picked it up and there was this remarkable voice on the other end of the line. An extremely attractive voice says 'Is Elizabeth there?' I said, 'No, she isn't. But who shall I say called her?'

It really was an attractive voice, the most intriguing I'd heard in a long, long time. The voice identified herself as Riane Eisler.

My instant reaction within myself was that this cannot be the Riane Eisler I know so well – never having met her, simply having formed this extremely negative image within myself! Intrigued by the contradiction between her voice and my image I kept her on the line. We chatted on and on and of course it wound up with the idea that we really ought to get together for lunch sometime soon. We met for the first time that weekend and I was a goner. I fell in love within a matter of a few hours, came back to her house about 4 a.m., dropped my first love poem through the mail slot, and from then on we were literally inseparable.

Why were we brought together? Why are we together now, and I would hope, in some way beyond understanding, forever? I believe it is simply because we were meant to be. I feel profoundly there was a non-chance element involved. The more I look at my life before meeting Riane and what has happened since in the lives of both of us the more I feel that Fate, Destiny, whatever you want to call it, most definitely brought us together, and for a specific purpose.

She was at a critical juncture in her life, in very poor health, having survived a near-death experience. Her book, *The Chalice and The Blade* – which I join Ashley Montagu in feeling is 'the most important since Darwin's *Origin of Species*' – lay as yet ahead. I was exactly the right person to come into her life at that time, to help rebuild her health, and to provide her with the support she needed for 10 years to write that book. She in turn out of the labor of those years provided me with an intellectual framework which made it possible for me to pull together my gropings and deep passionate surges in various directions and build my own work towards some potentially lasting contribution in the area of moral sensitivity. Psychologically, she also filled a great empty cavern within my psyche that made it possible for me to achieve the wholeness and the strength of mind and affection and will that was an unreliable factor in my life beforehand.

There is, I believe, an element of the psychic chosen, if you want to put it that way – a psychic connection that seems to emerge in deep, profound, and lasting love. It has long seemed to science a very romantic notion that you could have such a thing as star-crossed lovers or whatever the expression is. The idea that some special fate, some special destiny brings you together is everywhere pooh-poohed and of course has been disproved by hard-nosed sociological studies. But several things happened around the time we met that, as I've pondered them over the years, make me think differently.

Undercover, as most scientists these days are forced to do these things, I was engaged in psychic research at the time at UCLA. 'Upstairs' at the UCLA School of Medicine I was the research director of a large conventional project, but 'downstairs' (quite literally – in a room in the basement of the Neuropsychiatric Institute) I met every week for two years with a group scientifically exploring telepathy.

A few days after Riane and I met I took her to one of these Wednesday-night research sessions, and during the break a woman came up and said, 'Do you mind if I ask you something?'

'Go ahead,' I said.

'Last week you were here by yourself, weren't you?' she said.

'Yes,' I said.

'Do you know what happened? I looked over at you – I was sitting across the group from you and I looked over where you were sitting and I thought you looked very lonely.' Then her face brightened and she turned to look at Riane. 'And the moment that I thought that he was lonely I saw *you* sitting right next to him!'

Now the woman thought this was remarkable because she assumed that Riane was my wife or girlfriend and that she had had a telepathic experience. But the amazing thing here was that she had actually had a *precognitive* experience. Before I had actually met Riane – even before that first phone call that might have primed my mind in some way – this woman had seen her sitting next to me in this situation of unusual psychic receptivity.

I, too, had earlier had such an experience. About four months before I met Riane, back when she was nothing to me but this woman I'd decided to avoid and had dropped from mind, I was driving along one day feeling very desolate, lonely, there in the midst of all the sunshine and the perfect weather and the beautiful foliage. In effect I asked myself, or something within myself, Who am I looking for? What does she look like?

Rather quickly there came to me this image of a woman in her mid-forties, tall, slim, with curly, close-cropped hair and big glasses, very big glasses, and a sort of impish look on her face.

Now it was some weeks after we had met and I was already deeply in love when suddenly I recalled this earlier experience. I was thunderstruck by the fact that I had seen Riane before I knew her – for the earlier image was an exact fit to the later reality – simply by asking out of great need who is this ideal woman I am seeking, what does she look like?

What further impressed me as a psychologist was that if you were going strictly by the stereotype – here I was, a middle-aged guy, probably going through some kind of mid-life crisis, here in Los Angeles, the center of some of the most gorgeous women in the world – what would logically have popped up? Well, of course, I would have seen a young, voluptuous blonde in a bikini, the standard dream for those such as I. But instead I see this very different kind of woman, whom I had never seen before, not simply Riane, but I had never seen any woman, to my knowledge, who fitted that particular description, which she fit to a 'T'.

It was back in that time, before I knew her, that I also took a more conventional route to making connection. Before I met her, in that lonely state, going through dead-end affairs, I got to thinking surely there must be a way of short-cutting this miserable process. Here I was, a psychologist trained in *test development*. Wasn't there some kind of test I could develop to give to these women I met which would tell me rather quickly whether they were the right one?

Now while that may sound rather crazy, because it immediately conjures up this picture of this dorky psychologist hauling out a 300-question questionnaire at the first dinner out, in my case it actually made sense. My forte was in developing simple but powerful tests using what is known in the trade as the unobtrusive methods approach. I considered carefully my own psychodynamics, problems, childhood, traumas, etc., and came up with this single question as the key to happiness in relation to the whole realm of psychological requirements. The question would be 'Did you love your father?'

(The key relational problem I was trying to take care of here, familiar to others I'm sure, was that because of my mother's ambivalence and drive for domination I was, during conflicts, fiercely motivated to withdraw from women. This I knew must be offset by a mate motivated, through loving her father, not to withdraw but rather to seek reconciliation at such times.)

Then I considered all of the other things that we value in life – sunsets, sunrises, music, art, human relations, values, goals, all of that. And I found that I could reduce all this once again to a single question: 'Who is your favorite composer?'

I had fallen in love with her, and was having a wonderful time for about two weeks, when suddenly I remembered this test, which had completely dropped from mind during this blissful period. I thought to myself, Oh my God! To be true to my training and scientific self I must take the chance with this test. But what if she doesn't answer the questions right? What if she answers the questions wrong – and my love is so powerful that I am compelled to disregard the test? I decided that it was still worth taking the chance because if she answered the questions wrong this would at least be a signal that at some point this love, alas, like all others, would run into the usual obstacles and fade.

So I waited patiently – this is part of the unobtrusive methods approach – for the right situation to present itself and finally she got on the subject of her family. So I asked how did she feel about her father. She brightened and said quite simply and directly, 'I loved my father.'

Wonderful! She had passed half the test! But now came the crucial part. The right answer was Mozart. What if I asked her the question and she answered Tchaikovsky? This would be a serious problem, for Tchaikovsky was way down on my list except for one or two pieces. Beethoven might be a borderline consideration, but the more I thought about it Mozart was the real honest requirement. So time passed and we got into a discussion of classical music and I asked her very innocently, 'Who's your favorite composer?'

Again she brightened and said, 'Why, Mozart, of course.'

So that was it! I've always felt very good about this because it not only validated our love but validated my skill as a test developer.

As that song of some time ago put it, What is this thing called love? I guess I will always think of that first morning after we met and I went back over to her house and dropped my first love poem through the mail slot.

Thereafter, I wrote a poem, sometimes two, a day and they were the best things I'd ever written. They were expressing my love in its *context*, which is the important thing. Not in abstractions, but the love that comes out of the specific time, place, happening, and feelings, out of the living context. This had been going on for maybe three weeks and at some point in there Riane began to write letters back to me, even though we were seeing each other daily. Because these poems came out of this deep well of some self-transcendent source and were the best things I'd ever written, I naturally began to think of the possibility of publication some day.

I remarked to her that maybe there is a book here, a small book, someday, thinking of her letters also in reply to me.

She replied, 'Yes. And I know the title. *One Hundred Days of Love.*'

I said yes, that was a good title – but then I realized that this would commit me to write one hundred love poems day after day! This would be over three months of daily deadline pressures for that most elusive and delicate of art forms!

I said it would be impossible for me to feel enough of this surge over such a stretch as to every day write a poem that would be meaningful.

She looked at me in a whimsical way and with a smile said, 'You could if you really loved me.' So she had me hooked. I wrote a poem a day not simply for one hundred days but for some time beyond that, and I still write her poems every so often.

Contrary to how the cynical tab such small revelations, this was and is no trivial matter, for poetry is the language of love. Sometimes I think that if we are to understand love deeply we must either write or read and cherish poetry. Prose simply does not have the lift. 'The Song of Songs', Andrew Marvell, Heinrich Heine, Robert Burns – those simple lines of Burns', 'My love is like a red, red rose', so simple and yet what they lead to so right.

As fair thou art, my bonnie lass,
   So deep in love am I;
And I will love thee still, my dear,
   Till a' the seas gang dry.

Till a' the seas gang dry, my dear,
   And the rocks melt wi' the sun;
I will love thee still, my dear,
   While the sand o' life shall run.

And fare-thee-well, my only love!
   And fare-thee-well a while!
And I will come again, my love,
   Though it were ten thousand mile.

Never has so much that really matters been said so simply and directly, straight from heart and mind to heart and mind.

There are many sides to love, of course. There's this impression that since Riane's book, *The Chalice and the Blade*, has made the 'partnership way' charismatic, and since we have a book out we've done together, *The Partnership Way*, that we've found the secret of no conflict and are this 'ideal' couple who just bask in the happiness of being with one another all the time. Well, of course, that's completely unrealistic. We both have strong identities, very strong opinions. And I'm particularly stubborn. So naturally we can come to radical differences on certain things every so often. This leads to some rather intense arguments, which we resolve in a variety of ways, particularly the co-counseling approach Riane describes.

   Some conflicts never do get resolved, of course. I think this is something couples must honestly face up to. A problem in our life together is my tendency to procrastinate, putting things off 'until tomorrow' or leaving things half completed, like a drawer left open rather than fully closed. Riane feels she has no recourse but to finish it herself or 'bug' me. Likewise, there are times I feel she is being too demanding, or trying overmuch to control. Those problems persist, although we do manage to resolve them by heated exchanges that eventually evolve into tolerance.

Beyond all other methods for resolving conflicts, however, I think it is a sense of obligation to something larger than ourselves – a sense of, if you will, a mission together – that quiets and re-settles us when rage still erupts.

I don't think everybody is meant to work at the kind of intellectual, social, political, economic or spiritual task one might call a mission here on earth. I feel the idea is for all of us to do the best we can. And I feel that if two people find a special connectivity, if they achieve that in a lifetime, that is enough. That adds something very important to the thrust forward of evolution. In the case of Riane and myself – looking back at history and prehistory, and looking ahead into what I think I see of the future – I do feel, however, that we were given something special to do.

We've reached this particular juncture, all of us, in the evolution of our species where unless certain things change we may either wipe out the species or set the whole planet back by potentially thousands of years. I know many people see this quite clearly. To see that we are engaged in a great evolutionary transformation, that more and more of us are now working consciously toward this end – I think this is the exciting thing, where in the past whatever was done in this direction was unconscious, or there was only a tiny handful who consciously attempted to work with the evolutionary forces.

I think also in past times people have been hampered by not having the opportunity we have today. We have this rare opportunity to leap forward as a species. I feel that this is what gives the great additional lift to Riane and I having found each other and living and working together. We have picked our two tasks and are still young enough to put in some good years toward completion of these tasks or at least moving them significantly along. One is to accelerate the shift from a dominator to a partnership society. The other, closely allied, is my particular chosen effort, to develop a new understanding of moral sensitivity that makes it possible to bolster, clarify, strengthen and extend our present efforts in this urgent direction.

One cornerstone for the new theory of moral sensitivity that I'm developing is that moral sensitivity rises out of the drive, and dialectical relationship, of two forces running through all levels of life, which we know at the level of values as 'freedom' and 'equality'. This may seem awfully abstract and involved, but it's interesting to me to see how easily this part of the theory may be applied to everyday life, particularly in our own relationship to one another. That we expect to – and do – treat each other as equals is an easy, understandable fit. But what about freedom in a relationship? Obviously there must be limits – certain agreements we must reach together, not independently, without consulting the other. Riane can't invite someone over for dinner with no consultation, for example, for I'm the cook and am leery of involvement much beyond caring for our own needs. But there's another aspect to this freedom question, the need to not feel controlled or manipulated. William Blake said it well: 'He who would to himself bind a joy doth the winged life destroy.'

We both know firmly by now that we're going to go farther together than either one of us could have gone by ourselves. And in the process we'll greatly expand our enjoyment of life. I personally cannot conceive of any sustained enjoyment of life unless one has a sense of a sustaining higher purpose.

And yet I think if I had to choose between doing something significant in keeping with my present greatest dreams or spending the rest of my life with Riane – if I couldn't have them both – I would pick spending the rest of my life with Riane.

This, I would feel, would not only be by far the most pleasurable choice, but also in the long run the most significant.

I see this relationship as for life and, hopefully, beyond. I also, in all realism, see it as a monogamous relationship. I'm certainly tempted by the thought of straying at times. I find women enormously attractive. I've come to think that this is something more than just being heterosexual. I find women as a gender more interesting than men. I have good male friends, whose friendships I value and with whom I can feel at ease, but there is an undeniable depth and a exoticism that certain women have that appeals to me much more. As for monogamy, I see it partly as a matter of loyalty and partly as a matter of practicality. To relate deeply and intensely to more than one person would be too confusing, and why should I if I find in Riane everything in this direction I could wish?

Increasingly now, as we both grow older, I am intrigued by the spiritual dimension of our relationship: spirituality closely interlinked with love and also closely interlinked with sex. In all three there is this thread in common of connectivity, of the yearning for self-transcendence and a joining and rejoining with great primal forces out of which I feel we emerged originally, to which I increasingly feel we return.

I am currently, through the fascinating process of past lives regression, exploring the possibility of prior and future connections to Riane. I see this as in no way something only faddish, weird or gimmicky. I'm convinced there is something to it through several vivid experiences of this kind. I feel it is another part of this new movement to reconnect with the spirituality that has been denied us by our education and by science and by sophistication, by our fears of seeming naïve or old-fashioned: all these attitudes that are fortunately passing as we move into what Pitirim Sorokin saw as the shift from a sensate to an idealistic phase of cultural evolution.

Riane's projection of a shift from the dominator ethos to the partnership ethos is another perspective on the same phenomenon. In this case, however, she is – along with a favored set of other women, for the first time with some potential long-range impact historically – drawing upon the profound new charisma, power and numinosity of the long-suppressed feminine. The mainstream still tends to mock all this as just 'women's issues' or the 'Goddess cult', but behind it all lies the ancient power of the inbuilt human potential, denied and diverted, now once again rising out of the deep past, rising from our roots to reconnect us with the transcendent stream.

By seeking Riane in the past I hope to find the key to a way for our rejoining in the future. Rationally, of course, it seems impossible. But as we are all like children just beginning to learn to swim in relation to spirituality, I feel that by swimming out beyond the breakers, and plunging deep, and carefully noting what I see and comparing notes with other psychic and spiritual explorers, I may find the way.

It seems inconceivable that two people could meet and love deeply and build together something meaningful in this life and then that it should all dissolve with no remnant. It makes no sense economically, let alone spiritually. And yet even those who believe that our lives are in some way eternal tend to believe that the individual passes into the great mass of the oversoul, so that the chance of linking up again is probably minimal.

This may well be the way it is all put together. But I cannot accept it without trying to discover otherwise. Trying to find the way that we may meet and be together again and again and again.

Chloe Goodchild & Roger Housden

CHLOE GOODCHILD

My dreaming years were over. Past experience had shown me that I was destined neither to be a nun, nor a traditional wife. At 32, I was alone, and a new journey had begun. Someone deep down in my soul opened her eyes, took in a deep breath, and breathed out a long and satisfying sigh of relief. I carried with me three commitments: to inner freedom; to my daughters' well-being; and to a love of singing.

Meeting Roger at the outset of that journey was a magnificent and surprising thing. Here was a man, full of laughter and aliveness, a passionate and adventurous spirit, and, more important than anything, someone who listened to life in the same way. Here was an ally, and a mature companion. Roger's recent life story also bore remarkable similarities to mine. We were both part-time parents, having concluded our first marriages. This established a mutual understanding, a shared empathy with each other's plight and pain. Roger's son, Yann, is seven years older than my daughter Rebecca.

Some strange act of fate had directed us both to the same living accommodation. Roger had moved there some weeks before me. We were intimate strangers under the same roof. I had my room and Roger had his. We met in the kitchen. I played Bach and Mozart, Mahler and Messaien in my room, and he played ethnic music in his. We became vital company for each other, while also endeavouring to face the consequences of our recent actions with single-minded attention. What sustained and nourished us both during that time was this all-pervading stillness and joy which we encountered every time we came together. My increasing intimacy with Roger was like a deep aliveness which was present whatever we were doing. No push, no pull, no stay, no go. Simply being there together was rich enough.

Although I had been through many affairs in adolescence and early adulthood, I had only really known this shared presence with one other love 12 years previously in a relationship which took place across the Atlantic. Due to geographical difficulties and other circumstances beyond our control, that relationship never came to ground.

Sexuality had been a revelation to me as an adolescent and my first real orgasm at the age of 17 instilled a deep trust in my own body, its life and power. The sexual act for me is something which expresses and celebrates the widest range of feeling, from the animal instinctual to the transpersonal; from the desire-full to the desire-free. I know all this through and with Roger. When the silence which first 'held' us began to move us sexually. We simply followed it together, treading softly to begin with, then walking into valleys, rolling in warm grass, bathing in soft water, plunging into lakes, climbing mountains, jumping, soaring, laughing, crying, tearing through wildness, falling, cascading, exploding, dissolving, opening, receiving, delighting in flowers, resting in stillness – the images are endlessly changing.

Monogamy I should say, however, was not a high priority when my first marriage came to an end, prior to meeting Roger. Following the suffering and grief of that experience, I concluded sadly that I was not intended to have a single partner for life. All the time, there was a tension in me between 'the hermit' on the one hand, and Aphrodite, the creative/sexual transformer, on the other. The choice to be monogamous arose naturally out of the sexual dynamic between Roger and myself. Monogamy, like celibacy or becoming a vegetarian, cannot be an 'ought' or a 'should'-based choice. It's not even a choice, really. It simply chooses you or it doesn't. The context of my intimacy with Roger allowed that to happen. Whether or not sexual fantasies arise (and of course they do) I am aware that to disperse my sexual energy now, with additional 'galavantings', would disturb and dilute the vital energy that I use in my work. I derive such sexual satisfaction within my relationship with Roger that to pursue more elsewhere would clearly be greedy and a wasted displacement of attention.

What of the more shadowy aspects of our intimate relationship? Betrayal is a theme which has followed me all my life, since early childhood. I was born on Good Friday and have spent many years pre-occupied with that moment in the Garden of Gethsemane, when Christ received the kiss of betrayal with unquestioning acceptance. That has always fascinated and disturbed me. It was as if that 'mythic moment' opened the way to an unconditional love that I longed to find.

Alongside all the beauty and magic of the early stages of my relationship with Roger, I kept picking up on what seemed like Roger's adherence to an 'anima' figure (an image of idealized woman) that I did not represent for him. There were those moments when his gaze was directed elsewhere, and his body wanted its options to be left open. Two such potential 'options' were the magician/witch and the more assertive 'career woman' type, neither of which were foremost in my own psychic make-up at the time. So it was that I conspired against myself or, more correctly, Roger and I entered a conspiracy which simmered on for a while. I inwardly contracted from the company of such women when with Roger and secretly endeavoured to 'become' them, so as to offer Roger a partnership with *the total woman*. So, whenever Roger expressed a simple enjoyment of such women, I would immediately leap into mistrust. I wonder how many marriages/partnerships have broken up due to the repeated inability, or unwillingness, of both partners to 'see through' and disidentify with such dilemmas? 'You are never upset for the reason you think you are,' goes the saying. Yet, despite ourselves – possibly because habitual suffering is a more familiar and, therefore, paradoxically 'safer' place to be – we can tend towards self-destructive patterns of behaviour, rather than travel, with courage, into the unfamiliar territories of conciliation and resolution.

Self-betrayal is, of course, the most miserable form of suffering. The above scenario is an example of that. Not to listen to the leadings of one's own heart, and to live solely in the light and shadow of the other, has been a particularly key theme for many women given the expectations of our social conditioning. Certainly it is true that, at the beginning of my relationship with Roger, I was so consumed with love for and by him that I lost my own sense of self and made our relationship the one living reality. I idealized Roger, his physical beauty, eloquence, self-assurance and spiritual fervour. In truth, I embarked upon a narcissistic path, in which he and I were of one body. Of course there was truth in this. We had experienced through silence and passionate, sexual dance the many forms of alchemical interchange. Those moments when you are locked in one another's arms in ecstasy, and there is no knowing where one body ends and the other begins. This experience of 'oneness', however, protected me from the reality of my own authority and power, which I rediscovered later when Roger and I travelled to India. I will speak of that later. As time passed, my own individual authority slowly began to emerge out of the ashes and teachings of my first marriage. As I came to know Roger, and ceased to idealize him, he came to rest in our relationship more and more deeply, as did I.

This did not mean that we were without conflict. Take, for example, the children. Roger and I did not come together to give birth to children. The 'children' that we have procreated have been in the form of creative projects and ideas. However, we did bring two beautiful, strong and independently-minded children from our previous marriages: Rebecca, my daughter, now 10 years old and Yann, Roger's son, now 17 years old. Finding the most loving and most appropriate way to create a new family context has been one of our major sources of conflict. When I first knew Roger, it was very difficult for him to accept the amount of energy and time that I needed and wanted to give to Rebecca. Whether she has been physically present with me or not, I have expended most of my energy in a concern for her well-being. This is a natural 'parenting' phenomenon, whether your children live with you full time or not. However, Roger and I were out of phase on this one. At the beginning, my daughter spent much more time with us than Roger's son, who was older and more independent. My daughter was only just learning to talk when Roger and I met. Roger had seen his son through this earliest part of childhood and did not wish to actively involve himself in that process again. I, who have stronger 'nurturing' instincts than he, found myself torn between my allegiance to my daughter, on the one hand, and this unstoppable love-bond with Roger that I had welcomed, on the other. My heart and hands were full! This conflict was the subject of enormous tension for me in the early years and I often had the feeling that I was not doing anything well. I was a half-hearted mother and an exhausted lover.

As regards Roger's son, Yann, in the full flood of adolescence, his needs were for a warm family context to grow up in. There were times when I was simply overwhelmed by the wealth of needs that poured out of those early years. I am thankful to say that the generosity and tolerance of our children, as well as the maturing of time, has enabled the four of us to come to enjoy each other's company both as friends and as parents/children. I know of no other teacher as powerful and direct as our own children. They are likewise learning the lessons of communication and co-operation, which would otherwise be more difficult as single children.

The need for boundaries and private space has been another area of tension for me. Roger founded the Open Gate in 1986, when we had just bought and moved into our first house together (two years after our first meeting). The Open Gate has international telephone calls coming in at all times of the day and sometimes night. The office accommodated one part-time assistant, and was situated on the top floor of our house, next door to the bathroom. The telephone rang constantly. This lack of privacy began to jar heavily for me by the second year of the Open Gate's life, and it finally culminated in an exasperating and warfaring argument which went on all day, in a French chateau several summers ago. This conflict showed us the darkest and most unrelenting sides of our natures. A year later, the office moved out, which brought renewed breathing space all round. We both now love the distance between the home and the work scene. I love it especially when I have been working away a lot. I love the quiet and the privacy.

The departure of the office from our house was accompanied by a stronger nurturing quality between Roger and I. We began to give the house much more attention and loving care. We unblocked the chimney, opened up the fireplace and had a fire burning in the hearth for the first time. This 'earthing' activity was not given much attention in the early years. It has supplemented and balanced out the stimulating and 'on the edge' aspects of our relationship. So we are enjoying watching its harmonizing effect on our time with the children, and with our close friends. As Roger has come to appreciate this new sense of privacy at home, I now have to watch the degree to which my music projects, album production meetings, and so on – which often take place at home – accord with *his* threshold of tolerance. Anger and explosions can suddenly arise with unimagined force between us, if that threshold is stepped over at home. Yet this endless play of swings and roundabouts, giving and receiving, is the grist out of which has arisen a deepening respect for each other's pace and space.

For us, the pleasure which we have experienced in so many ways – not just sexually, but walking together, singing, dreaming, playing, eating, dancing, travelling – have all opened the door ever wider on our desire for that freedom of unconditional acceptance which is the ground of intimate relationship. We sang, we read books, we ran groups together, we played and argued with our children, we met key people whom we hoped would bring us closer to the truth about ourselves, we made love some more, we meditated, we did relationship exercises . . . and so it went on, these 'soul-building' exercises, until finally, we decided to go to India. This was not the romantic notion that it may sound. My motivation was also fuelled by my increasing involvement in Indian vocal music, together with a significant connection that I had made with a twentieth-century woman saint called Sri Ananda Mayi Ma. She had died in 1982, nevertheless the impact of her unconditional Being upon my life with Roger, our children and my work, was enormous. So I was very keen to seek out people who had known Her and received Her teachings.

Our visit to India in January 1990 was a unique turning-point for Roger and me. It brought with it a death and a rebirth. For me, it was a death of all the residual and binding projections that I had subtly placed upon Roger. A death of my dependence on him as the outer expression of my 'inner male'. A death of the narcissistic attachments fuelled by the 'need to merge' physically in order to be complete, and to maintain our 'coupleness'.

What happened? How did this come about? As with our first meeting, grace intervened. This time it was in the form of an old man, whose current of love enveloped us and catalysed this initially fierce transformation. The impact of this process struck me first. That is to say it dissolved the obstacles – the desires, thoughts and impressions of my reactive mind – and revealed a quality of being, self-awareness and containment such as I had never known. This enabled me to 'see into' my relationship with Roger with renewed clarity, authority and detachment. I was able to be with him and gaze upon him without any trace of condition or expectation. Indeed, the whole of life around me opened itself up in this way. The experience of 'oneness' that I had been seeking with, and through, Roger was suddenly everywhere. Everything passed through me. I was as intimately joined with the flowers in the Botanical Gardens in Lucknow, the traffic, the wind and the noise of India, as I was with Roger. Nothing mattered. Everything was as it was. I could see my thoughts and feelings pass like dust through the air. I could also see Roger's suffering and his fear that something very dear had suddenly gone.

In the days that followed this experience, it was extremely difficult to share with Roger the deeper intimacy that I had entered into with him and with life itself. His reactions for and against my state of being were often wild, and uncontrollable. Gradually, though, this inner fire began to grow in him also, and we began to enter a new dimension of togetherness. Now we were faced with the realization that our choice to remain together was no longer fuelled by projection, conditioning, need, or a specific social story-line. Such factors were irrelevant. Food for the birds. As the months passed and our ordinary personalities reasserted themselves, we began to realize that life had united us in the simplest, most profound way. There arose a choiceless inseparability about our lives together. This was no mental or romantic notion, but an unselfconscious, shared knowledge that the very muscle and cells of our bodies were dancing together. At the same time, we were more aware of our aloneness now and our own individuality than we ever were. Our time in India returned us to ourselves in the same moment that it forged a potent bond between us.

I have always loved to be alone. Every now and again, either Roger or I take a few days and travel away from home. I love to be completely alone or, if with others, in a meditation context so that the attention is gathered inwards and there is no need for sociability. My favourite place is a tiny boat-house on the River Dart close to Dartmoor in Devon. We both love aloneness at home too, so we each have our own bedroom, on a different floor. This means that we can choose when we want to sleep together. It takes any potential 'habitualness' out of that ritual. It ensures that we can meet in bed either with fresh passion or with the simple wish to lie side by side, gently held. There is a lively energy created too by the unpredictability of knowing whether or not you are going to sleep alone.

Laughter, playfulness and pleasure form an integral part of our lives too, as does the love of silence and a shared spiritual language. That language has shifted and changed quite dramatically since we first met. The language of 'spiritual longing' has diminished and simplified as our own needs have been met through the mirror we have presented to each other since our journey to India. Similarly with our shared sexual language, the line between what was previously 'sacred' or 'sexual' has faded. They are intrinsic to each other, two aspects of the selfsame tree.

The child spirit is something that we strongly encourage and with it the love of play and adventure. It pervades all our activities and brings with it unexpected tricks and wild imaginings. So often in relationships this spirit remains only for the period of 'novelty', the so-called 'honeymoon' phase. To my surprise, this experience of novelty and of eros has never left us. I guess this is because we do not take each other for granted. Unpredictability and changing patterns bring vitality. The danger, of course, with the 'eternal child' is that s/he is often only interested in the beginnings of things, with the upturning of stones and tables. My experience often in previous relationships was that when the novelty wore away, only a kind of lukewarm resignation or a weighty sense of responsibility remained. Here with Roger, however, I experience both the unpredictability of the child spirit and the depth of a life generated by two maturing adults.

As for commitment, it is for me a choiceless 'knowing' that we are fundamentally inseparable. This knowing is felt in the cells of the body and is beyond personal wish or romance. Our commitment is to that presence that I have spoken of, rather than to each other. That presence has become more potent as our relationship has progressed. So the question for me is more what is the quality of that presence which, when we are receptive to it, dissolves questions of doubt, like or dislike, between us? Our commitment is to living in the present and in that 'presence'. That, for me, brings an implicit strength and security with it into the relationship rather than the insecurity which comes with planning ahead and trying to place a time factor on our life together.

Making a formal statement of marriage has not seemed relevant to us yet. We do fantasize occasionally about a special ceremony. It will no doubt arise naturally when the time beckons. Neither of us have a hankering to state our love in front of a public witness. If such a statement is needed, this chapter must be it.

ROGER HOUSDEN

This is embarrassing. I have to admit that at the age of 30 my knowledge of woman could still be written on a postage stamp. That, of course, is to say that great tracts of my own soul remained uncharted, and still now there are territories I can barely give a name to. For much of my twenties and thirties I was embroiled in a relationship which was fundamentally unsuitable for both of us; and I fell wildly in love with a woman whom circumstances made unavailable. I was in my thirties before I began to have fulfilling erotic relationships with women who I could see as real people rather than sex objects or projections of my own fantasies. All, however, was not lost. I know now that the various liaisons of my earlier life, including the most transient and unconscious ones, were always part of a larger mosaic; and every one of them has in some way had an integral part to play in leading me both to myself and to my life with Chloe.

There is not one of them I do not remember, even the sight of a face in a nightclub when I was 18 – a face that haunted me for weeks. Some of these women I know I shall never forget. With one person in particular, doors were opened onto a world of psychic union and onto a whole range of feelings I had never known existed. For this last, especially, and for every woman I have ever known, I feel a deep and lasting gratitude. Men have been important in my life, too, as friends, as teachers, and as agents of the spirit; but in being agents for the revelation of my own soul, women have led me toward myself as much as any spiritual or psychological discipline has; and they have brought me to the relationship I find myself in now, the consummation of my experience of intimacy.

I first met Chloe when I was 40. I was renting a room in the house of a friend, after leaving my marriage. I was relieved and happy to be on my own, and the last thing I was looking for was another partner. Several weeks later, my friend said that she was considering renting another room in her house, and that someone who was interested in it would be ringing to make a time to meet me. The person wanted to know who she might be sharing a house with. A week later, the phone rang, and this sonorous voice, resonant as a bell, came ringing down the line. When I heard it, something in me felt like laughing and crying at the same time. I had come here to be alone; but already, I could hear that life was not going to go as I had planned.

Chloe duly moved in, and in doing so, she, too, was leaving her marriage and her child. She came with great sadness, but even so, her huge spirit filled the house with life and laughter. The laughter was what I remember most of those first meetings at breakfast, which, to begin with, was the only time we would meet. She always had a kind of glow, a sunny aura; it was like having champagne breakfast without having to buy champagne. This was more than just fun, though; we became very available to each other and, gradually, I came to realize that this was someone by whom I felt met at the profoundest level. The years that have passed since then have only confirmed and deepened that feeling. Our life together is a passionate and vital one, physically, mentally and emotionally. There is an inherent aliveness between us which gives us great pleasure, often joy, in the other's company. At the same time, there is a quietness which comes from being able to rest in the other's presence, and in a shared silence. A quiet and constant passion, one not determined by outer events, is at the heart of our togetherness.

We have lived together for seven years, which is both a very short and a very long time; time enough, though, for me to realize that, whatever may happen, there is no going back on the path of love. Along that path we have crossed many terrains, including some stretches of stony ground. Along with our enjoyment of each other, we have had our share of conflict at times, over issues both large and small. There was, for example, the story of the sorbet. That was a morning when I felt in my prime. Everyone knows the kind: the occasions, not always common, when one feels life is in hand, when things are happening when and how they were meant to (according to plan, that is to say). Chloe and I had arranged to meet for lunch at a favourite restaurant. We talked our way happily through the main course, obviously enjoying each other's company. I did not want a dessert, and Chloe ordered a sorbet. Now what came back was no spoon of ice in some tarnished metal cup, but three scoops of sorbet stretched out from the rim of a dinner-plate and all converging on a centre, adorned with a sprig of mint. Around and between the sorbet peninsulas was a thin lake, half of it cream, the other half a dark fruit syrup. Chloe saw as soon as I did that I was inclined to partake of this paradise, and she guided a spoon of sorbet in the direction of my mouth. As the spoon grew nearer, I could see that what I was really wanting was not on it, the cream and the syrup. So I took the spoon from her hand, scooped it into the lake on the plate, and from there into my mouth. In one fell swoop, all notions of paradise were scattered to the wind. Chloe felt that her offering to me had been taken over; that I had effectively negated it by taking more. She felt my action to be invasive, and I protested that I had no idea why she should be so upset.

My arm had moved to the plate without my knowing whose arm it was; for the deep waters had parted, and onto the lunch table had sprung the demanding children we once were, and are still, all without any forewarning. A pall hung over the table until we left. We were not quick enough that time to see who was relating to who.

Occasionally we are so determined to be in the right or not to lose face that an argument can simmer on for days. More often, we remember our love for each other in the midst of it all and everything falls into perspective. Humour can cut the knot, and so can the readiness to feel and communicate the origins of our distress, which rarely have much to do with the particular situation in hand. Not infrequently, mummy and daddy are to be found lurking in the shadows.

Though conflict is not common for us, it can arise over anything, as the sorbet shows all too plainly. Most often, though, it is in some way connected to our children. Chloe has a daughter of 10, Rebecca, and I have a son of 17, Yann. Neither of them have their main home with us, though both of them are with us frequently. As a large proportion of the population knows, being a visiting child and being a step-parent are not easy tasks. Three or four different worlds are being asked to mesh, often in a short space of time. As a four, it can often feel piecemeal and dispersed: guilt arises, conflicts of need and interests emerge, as do jealousy, betrayal, love and hate. We are learning to work our way through what at times can seem like a minefield – laid, we are realizing, not only by our children, but equally by ourselves.

My particular challenge has been to say a full yes to Rebecca – to give her my real attention, and the feeling that I value her presence. It has taken me a few years to embrace her as part of my life with Chloe, whom one part of me, I have come to acknowledge, has wanted all to myself (as Rebecca has too, of course.) Rebecca lives with her father, a few doors away, and in the past I was also resistant to the feeling of being tied to our present locality because Chloe and Rebecca needed to be near each other. I have come to recognize this feeling of being tied as part of a broader and older anxiety about being held down, and commitment in general.

I have always felt deeply committed to my relationship with Yann, however, and my loyalty to him has sometimes felt in conflict with my loyalty to Chloe – a conflict of attention, more than anything else. Chloe has felt the same with regard to Rebecca and me. Both our children are encouraging me to extend beyond the shell of my own self-preoccupation, and

I am gradually getting the message. I can truthfully say, though, that I am now enjoying them hugely; and, especially since my attitude to Rebecca has shifted, they contribute much richness to my life with Chloe – which does not mean that the difficulties do not continue.

What I have been describing are the ripples that scatter suddenly over a lake when some unknown creature stirs below the surface. Our everyday life together, with its clashes of drum and cymbal, its laughter and its consistent sharing of enjoyment, projects, worries, ideas, meals, baths, bills, dreams and toothpaste, all this daily exchange takes its course against an inescapable, background sensation that 'somewhere, down there, our boat has struck against a great thing'. That 'great thing' lives not in our personal unconscious – that domain of forgotten memories that lurches to the surface when one or the other of us dangles the right bait – but in the deeper, more impersonal layer where images and sounds have given way to silence. Whatever meaning we ascribe to our relationship has its roots down there. I may try to mythologize it by saying we are on some ancient journey together; that we have some task or work to accomplish here, or that we were 'meant' to come together in this life through the benevolence of fate. This may or may not be so, but, in essence, the rock we have struck together down there in the depths has no name. All I know is that waters spring from it.

It will tell us, then, where it wants to take us, not the other way around. It has its source in something other than my will or Chloe's, though our wills certainly have a part to play. It is as if there are three of us, Chloe, myself, and something other, drawn from each of us but larger than either. It is this third presence, tangible though unnameable, which unites us; and I would say that the degree to which we live in this, rather than any shared beliefs or practices, is what determines whether or not our relationship is a spiritual one from one day to the next. We are united in some way that is more solid than anything

I can touch. That union has its origins in the timeless domain, beyond personal history; but its effects reach down into the tangible events of our everyday life.

The everyday is not a weight to bind the wings of love. On the contrary, it can bring that love into the cells of the body, and test it with our feet of clay, rather than restricting it to some transpersonal stratosphere. I love our ordinary, everyday world; it is the ground where we find our true mettle; where we discover the depths of companionship, and learn to accept our own as well as each other's craziness. Our everyday foibles are what prevent us from generating a personal cult of two and turning our relationship into an idol. How can you make an idol out of a relationship in which one person is usually on their dessert before the other is half way through their first course; or in which one always finds something extra to take care of just as they are leaving the house, while the other is sitting in the car with the engine running? I am even beginning to see it as a sign of natural abundance when Chloe turns the bath taps on and returns half an hour later.

And in the midst of the everyday minutiae of a life together, there are realizations which persist as living presences, and which give meaning and substance in a continuous way. One such 'story' whose presence lives on in us both is this. In 1990, as a result of meeting an old man in India, our relationship underwent a death and a rebirth. The various levels of co-dependency we had become used to as an automatic part of our life together were dislodged overnight. Our mutual projections fell away, and each of us was returned to ourselves, though Chloe in advance of me. The first result of this was that Chloe effectively withdrew the image she had cast on me of her own inner masculine nature. She was no longer tacitly expecting me to live out the masculine for her, and so the power she had given me previously in that way suddenly evaporated. This was hardly easy for me; suddenly, along with the feelings of liberation and joy in seeing the fulfilment of my partner, I felt unnecessary.

There was a look in Chloe's eyes that made me feel no more or less loved by her than anyone else.

Now I had always been the one in this relationship, and in previous ones, to move from the personal to the impersonal, especially when it suited me, and allowed me to avoid confrontation, or to stay in control. This was very different; Chloe's gaze was self-sufficient without being disconnected. In between my feelings of abandonment, I could not help recognizing that, in Chloe, the reactive mind seemed to have suspended operation. Whatever upsurges of anxiety arose in me, she retained a rare equanimity, a presence that felt wholly unconditional. I can only emphasize that what happened to us at that time was not a deliberate procedure, some therapeutic work we consciously embarked upon. It was a matter of energy, catalysed by our meeting with an external agent, a benign-looking grandfather in his eighties. After that meeting, Chloe lay awake for nights, as clear as crystal and burning with some intense inner heat which caused her to sweat without ceasing; a heat that, among other things, burned her dependency on our relationship away. Then, in the following weeks, I lived through nights of alternate ecstasy and torment until something snapped in me as well, as if a piece of elastic that had been stretched taut for decades had suddenly been snipped through.

Through that experience, we are both more alone and more intimately together than we ever were. For others, the same might happen in the most simple and ordinary ways. In our case, the drama we invoked was doubtless a comment on our characters. For the first two or three years of living together we were like twins, cleaving to the joy and pleasure of our merging. Everyone, after all, likes to merge, even longs to, despite the fear that holds them back. This was true for us, as well, and the enchantment of the lovers' garden held us enthralled for some years. It is still a place we love to go to. Even so, we had always needed time apart, time to dream our own dreams and entertain our private wonderings. When the sword came to part

us, though, it was unexpected in its decisiveness and finality.
I have no doubt that its origins were in the deeper layers of our
own psyches. Somewhere, below our daylight minds, we were
wanting it. When it came, then, we recognized it, felt its pain,
and submitted to its power. We are alone now even when we
are together, though not in a way that makes us separate from
each other. I look at Chloe sometimes and marvel at how utterly
other she is to me. The paradox is that now we are at home
in our aloneness, we are joined in a way that is more complete
than before. Rather than being submerged by our union, our
individuality is enhanced by it.

None of this means that our personal histories do not still
call the tune and have us at each other's throats over a sorbet.
Nor does it mean we do not feel disconnected at times; or that
we do not tend the other way and prop each other up
occasionally. The thought still comes that we should end it all
now and channel the energy required for relationship into
individually fulfilling and creative endeavours; that life is simply
too short to spend years in the labyrinth of relationship. But
these wrangles have little power; they do not shake the deeper
ground. As for our individual expressions and endeavours, it is
evident that, far from being a distraction, our relationship is an
inspiration for them; while they in turn bring a richness to our
life together. The more each person is following their own
particular loves and dreams in life, the more of themselves they
have to bring to the other – if, that is, their dreams are
compatible and not pulling in different directions. If people are
going to share their lives with each other, they need first and
foremost to share a common 'story'. In our case, though the
details will vary and the surface expressions may be different,
the major themes and dreams that shape our responses to life
are very similar.

Do we think alike, then, on the themes of commitment and
marriage? Over time, something has been forged between us
which is unchangeable. Rather than being something I have had

to decide upon, then, commitment is more of a *de facto* condition, an expression of the nature of our togetherness. It is not a commitment to a contract or a list of rules; it is a willingness to honour an invisible bond. That translates into everyday life through my intent to encourage and further Chloe's own fullness along with my own. My seal is upon the dynamic process of the relationship, and not on a model of it that I have fixed in my head. My commitment is not a security, in the sense that I can expect something always to be there in the form I have known it. It is a challenge to ride with Chloe into the unknown in a direction that is unlikely to be of our conscious choosing. I am firmly in that saddle now, though not always without trepidation. After all, we may come across any number of strange creatures at some unsuspected turn of events.

That, however, is part of the package. It is not just to Chloe's fair and sunny face that I am wed; nor, I think, is she with me for my blue eyes only. Not to pour water on the first sign of fire, though not to start fires for the sake of it: that, I think, is our mutual response to trouble down below. For most of us, trouble down below usually erupts in the genitals. I have said that the shape of our relationship may change, but as far as I can see, our bond is, and is likely to remain, a monogamous one. That does not mean I am not awakened by one female form or another almost any day of the week; the turn of the head, the delight in feminine beauty, all that remains; but the momentum, the drive to make contact, has moved from foreground to background. Until our meeting with the Indian grandfather, I had felt watched over by Chloe somehow. It was as if she was immediately aware whenever my attention was taken by another woman. This fuelled my fear of being trapped and my wandering attention even more, and to some degree we were caught in an enclosed circle of reaction which neither of us wanted but neither seemed able to escape from. On our return from India, I was immediately aware that Chloe's eyes were no longer on me. The circle had been broken. It was not that she no longer cared; it was that, without any effort, she was caring in a different way – in a way that left me free to live my life as I pleased. The consequence was that, though I felt a great relief and liberation within the dynamic of the relationship, my attention was also more on her than ever before. From then on, my hankering to feel that, even in theory, the door was ajar has passed away from our life.

There also comes a time to make choices about where one directs one's attention. I have other challenges to meet now than those which are evoked by the danger and excitement of affairs, and I neither need nor wish to disperse myself in that way. More importantly, there is a way in which the alchemical bond between us makes the idea of other liaisons an irrelevancy. Whatever the unknown may hold in store for us, though, I trust our relationship to be spacious enough to allow any fires that may spring up to follow their course without either of us becoming too burned. A prerequisite for that is honesty, and it is important for us to communicate even the fantasies that one or the other of us may have.

It is also hard to imagine making love with another because I am already wholly fulfilled with Chloe. Our sexual life is as much of a delight now as it ever was, if not more so. Time is essential for any deep sexual communion; not just the span of making love itself, but the necessity of knowing someone over and through time. It is over time that we come to divulge our various sensibilities and vulnerablities; it is over time that trust grows. Through the sexual union, as all true lovers know, every plane of human existence can be made available; and not, I believe, through technique so much as an orientation of mind, an attitude of openness, awe and play. Making love for us is an act of strength and an act of surrender, of vigour and great tenderness; of listening, of silence, of speaking; of surprise, astonishment even, and unpredictability; of tears, of laughter and of deep rest; of the dark, instinctual forces of our mysterious carnal nature, and the radiance of the life that breathes us all. It is, of all acts, the act in which we stand revealed.

I see that kind of intimacy to be the purpose and centre of our life together; and though it may be most commonly generated in making love, it is not, in itself, limited to any one act or event. Rather, it is the space itself in which any act can take place, and within which the relationship itself can unfold. It is the third presence I have already mentioned. Though its touch will often come unsolicited, we need periodically to make ourselves wholly available to it, and a day or two a month we step away from our everyday life and environment and let the being of our relationship emerge and soak us again. That being is genuine intimacy, the third presence we feel bound to follow. In his poem, 'September 8th', Pablo Neruda says,

> Between you and me a door is opened
> And someone, still faceless,
> Was waiting for us there.

Though we have made no public or legal declaration of marriage, there is no question that we are already wedded in some interior alchemy that cannot be undone. I have never known this before, although I was previously married legally and publicly. The matter of a public marriage has raised itself every now and then, but it has never seemed to gather much will around it. I am not sure it goes too well with our natures; and our union is not a social one that especially needs to find its place on our family trees. It is a living tree of its own that probably even draws creative juices from its outsider status. We are certainly not together to procreate children, and the pressure to conform that pregnancy brings is not a consideration we expect to contend with. Our previous marriages have bequeathed us the joys and pains of parenthood, and we feel that our offspring will be of the creative imagination rather than of the flesh. What can I tell you? For good or for ill, for better or for worse, Chloe is already my great love and joy. I could not dream of a finer companion to be on this adventure with.

Eve Penner Ilsen & Zalman Schachter-Shalomi

EVE PENNER ILSEN

How do I dare to write about this? Zalman and I have been together only a few years. Some days I am certain that we will be together for the rest of – one of our – lives; other days I wonder what in heaven's name I am doing here at all. One thing is for sure, though: this is the first time in my life I have felt such a commitment to a person, a relationship. In times of great frustration, I roar at the commitment itself: how dare you keep me here, slogging through this? In times of clarity and calm, when I glimpse the whole with a bit of perspective, I smile in contentment that we have seen it through this far. In times of intense joy and delight, none of this crosses my mind.

We come to each other from opposite sides of the zodiac, across a difference of 24 years, two continents, and vastly different life experiences. He is rich with children, grandchildren and former marriages. I am childless, never married. The pattern of my life has been irregular, to say the least; and I stepped into a relationship embedded in the complexity of pre-existing conditions. There is such a roiling of richness between us that sometimes the sheer chaos threatens to overwhelm me. But then it occurs to me that one year, in my longing and praying for a deep soul partner, I may have added the foolish clause: 'And please, dear God, don't let me be bored.' As we know, God has a sense of humor.

My adoptive father, *olav ha-sholom*, used to say that, for one moment, God snatches away your common sense, and in that moment you fall in love, and that's it. My mother and he were gloriously happy in their marriage for 16 years, until his death. Every year around the time of their anniversary my mother would begin to discuss whether they should renew their contract; and of course, every year they would. (By the tenth year, he began to ask, rather plaintively, 'When do I get tenure?') I begin to understand that there is wisdom in this arrangement, as I find we seem to be continuing with a variation of my family tradition. We are in what Zalman has called a 'sacred, committed relationship'. Our underlying intent is that we remain together. Equally, there is a strong commitment that each of us lives out of the deep truth of his/her destiny and heart. We hold these commitments simultaneously and are challenged, when they seem to conflict, to look deeper, to extend patience, to face our own shadows and unknown places. This commitment to one's deep self is *not* a commitment to ease or comfort, but rather the reverse. It is an obligation to hear and to stand by one's own truth, which, more often than not, can be very uncomfortable. My teacher, Mme Colette Aboulker-Muscat, once remarked: 'If you are serious about spiritual development, you must learn to live with uncertainty.' So surely something good must be happening!

(Wait a minute, here. Wasn't it all supposed to fall into peaceful and predictable place once I met the man of my dreams? House and kids and all? Financial security? Someone *else* to deal with the plumber? Growing herbs and baking bread and quietly listening to the crickets together? Hah!)

In those prayers for the right partner, the one element that has remained constant, since my early adolescence, has been the wish to share a spiritual life. In this, She has been exceedingly generous – with a sense of humor. We assume God's presence, though what each of us means by that word may differ from the popular (deteriorated) version, and perhaps from the other's. One of Zalman's qualities most dear to me is his love of God, which keeps a steady pulsating beam beneath outward events and appearances. It is this reality, which never really wavers, no matter what a mess it looks his life is in, that attracts so many people to him, that potentiates his blessings, that does the actual work, whatever words happen to be coming out of his mouth. It is his most essential self, the core that I love so deeply. When I turn to regard my own relationship to God, I find I often tell myself that the lines are blocked, there is distance, no communication; God is there, just not accessible to me. When I sneak a look behind the veil, however, I find myself eavesdropping on what is practically a constant, ongoing communication; somewhere, I am always talking to God. And it is just possible that on some channel God is always communing with me. It occurs to me that this feels familiar: it is very much like the commitment to our relationship that is a quiet, invisible constant, a *basso continuo* while we sing the dramatic arias about whether this is viable. It is this longing for the heart of the universe that draws us to each other.

It is also the heart of our work, separately or together. Surely we would not have had the courage to take each other on as work partners, and to take on such a challenge as a Wisdom School, if we had only known . . .

We approach things so differently, we see them differently, we do them differently. A typical exchange might be:
Z: 'Okay, let's sit at the computer and work out the schedule.'
E: 'We can't do the schedule yet! We need to sort through the content in depth and find the organic *shape* it wants to take!'
Or, while leading a seminar:
E: (*sotto voce*) 'Time for a break.'
Z: 'But I still have four worlds, ten sephirot and three Hassidic masters to get through.'
E: 'Zalman, they need to pee.'
Z: 'Oh, all right . . .'
E: (loud) 'Okay, everybody, bladder break! We resume in 20 minutes.'
Z: 'Five!'
E: 'Ten!'
We are always bargaining, like fruitsellers at the shuq or Abraham with God. (Well, all right, a very slight exaggeration.)
I do tend to want to know the deep organic structure of our

teaching, the intent and the sequence and the flow; I want it to have an integrity of content and form and feeling. But Zalman's preference, and great talent, is for flying with the inspiration of the moment. People now tell us that we have created a remarkable balance when we work together. If so, this was achieved by struggle which has been loving, furious, enlivening, exhausting, gratifying, frustrating and has left us triumphant and bedraggled. Whose idea was this, anyway?

Were it not for the love between us, surely one of us would have declared our being and working together sheer insanity by now. Perhaps it is, anyway; but I begin to see that our love is the temptation, the bait, that keeps us sniffing, interested, persistent, obstinate even. What an ingenious arrangement. Because, in the meanwhile, what is going on? Why, my very most flagrant charactistics are being challenged, abraded, thwarted! I, who so value excellence in my (and others') work that I scare myself out of doing *anything*, am linked to a man who will let any old slipshod thing pass (I think) and hope for the best. He has no sensitivity, I tell myself, no discrimination. Aarghhh! 'Deeper, better, more elegant!' I scream. 'Will you please stop trying to control so much?' he counters. I can't believe he doesn't see the flaws I see. He can't understand what I'm making such a bloody fuss about.

In a general way, these caricatures are true: I am judgemental and critical and also have a good sense of discrimination and taste. He is generous and accepting and compassionate, and can also be sloppy. On the whole, I see that his way has more kindness. At worst, it can appear to others, and even to ourselves, that he is Father Compassion himself, and I am the Red Queen: 'Off with their heads!'

This business of being so much in the public eye poses difficulties. I would have assumed that our private relationship is private, but it is not; it is in full view. (Obviously, as a direct result of being so visible, we were invited to write this, and make the inside story *completely* public.) Shifting gears from the public face to the private one is not automatic. Will the *real* Zalman please stand up? Or lie down (with me)?

Nothing drives me more berserk, or leaves me feeling more betrayed, than the least little bitty shade of untruth from Zalman's lips. Yet most clergypeople seem to learn, for the sake of survival, a technique of softening unpleasant truths (often beyond recognition) so as to avoid direct confrontation. I think to myself: quintessentially Leo male, royally self-reverent and pussyfooting at the same time. At such a gambit I naturally leap forth with a furious yell, all my heavy confrontational artillery at the tip of my tongue. There ensues a pitched battle, in which each of us perseverates in using the precise strategy that most drives the other up the wall. The object here is not to win, but to come to some sort of understanding. So, over time, Zalman has learned the importance to me of impeccable truth; and his tolerance for passion of expression has increased. I have learned something of the importance to him of more kindness, of time and space to sort things out. He's doing better at this than I am.

I occasionally dream of discovering rooms in my house I had not known were there. These days, they are airy and cosy and full of beautiful, interesting or quirky things. The new spaces opening in me, at least in my work, have flowered in response to Zalman's presence in my life. He has invited and challenged me to use all of the skills I have ever developed in a new context, applied to material I had not dealt with professionally before, with a different group of people than are usually drawn to my own work. He has made space for me to expand, to risk, to try new and unfamiliar things. He has encouraged me and taught me. And I have had to see past my tentativeness, and acknowledge what skills and wisdom of my own I bring to him. Perhaps I had never realized before what I had to give. A certain expansion of self goes on for both of us in each other's presence. Both of us are multifaceted people. We have many and varied aspects, interests and skills. We are different ages all at once: we embody a certain timelessness.

Thank God, in Zalman I found a playmate. I don't take for granted that we engage each other in so many areas: intellectually, emotionally, heartfully; in spiritual longing and worship and practice; in love of this life, openness, curiosity, outrageousness, daring, gregariousness. We interest and excite and challenge and inspire each other. He makes up silly songs. We laugh a lot. (Without a sense of humor, we would never survive each other.) He forgets jokes after a while, so I can tell the same ones all over again. We play three-dimensional tic tac toe or hangman on paper mats while waiting at restaurants. We talk to strangers at airports. We try out different languages. I especially appreciate the subtleties of Hebrew, the etymology of roots, and Zalman's great skill and talent as a linguist. We have been known to take scholarly Hebrew books to bed with us because they were too exciting to put down. (Zalman calls this Jewish foreplay.)

But the *real* story goes on deeper beneath the surface. There is something about being so warmly *loved* that supports and frees me to discover who I am and who I might become. This is one expression of Zalman's compassionate heart; and when turned on me so fully and so personally, this love pervades my life. It is in the flow of my love for him that I am carried a little beyond myself. There remains no sense, as in the past, that I am waiting for my life to begin. I am fully involved, and therefore fully at risk.

On frustrated and grumpy days, I suspect Zalman of not seeing at all who I really am. At other times I wonder whether my definitions of 'myself' are not beside the point entirely. In the middle of sleep, sometimes, Zalman will turn, not waking, and murmur 'I love you' with such feeling in his voice that in my own sleep I hear this. It touches my heart, and soaks down deep to the roots and makes a quiet, ongoing healing of old pain and self-doubt and loneliness.

The Zalman that I love sometimes seems to have nothing whatever to do with the describable qualities of the outer man.

I feel at those times that I simply *know* this person; and I love him unconditionally, outside of space and time, where I am a friend of his well-being. In the midst of wrangling over our unmet needs, I find that, as a special grace, one or the other of us may drop into that place of unconditional love, where self-interest is not.

Of course, there remains the question of the unmet needs. I find it odd that at the time in my life when I am most *with* another, I am forced for the sake of the relationship towards more self-sufficiency. When it became clear that we needed to work more separately (after all that work it took to learn how to work together), I felt it as a physical effort to wrench my energy back into my own stream. It took over half a year. And now I have a strong urge to plunge into my own creative expression head-on. We dare not let our arrangements become static. There are rhythms of apart and together that have a life of their own, and I am trying to learn to read them like one reads river currents, overcoming my own reluctance to abandon predictability. How much intensity? How much time together/apart? We are still learning. Our wishes don't always coincide. We each need intimate contact *and* solitude. We need to work together *and* to work alone. We need our friendships with others, when not every 'other' is appreciated by our partner. My own tendency is to pour myself into all that is 'together', and let the rest live on the crumbs. But this suffocates the relationship. I see that each of us must commit seriously to his/her own lifestream, if the relationship is to survive.

(But I *wanna* cook for him and keep house and mend sweaters and be there for kids and listen sympathetically and organize his life and wear sexy nighties and be the heart of his household and always know when and how to say the wise and right thing because we know men's egos are fragile, and when I was growing up this was supposed to be the most satisfying life a woman could have. Of course, while training me for that, my mother also insisted that I could and should do anything I love and develop my own talents. And she was – is – a model of lively outrageousness herself. I got a perfectly clear double message. But this seems to be the nature of the time. Both are true and neither are true, and no one model works unmodified. Zalman, with his Eastern European Orthodox/Hassidic background, has made huge shifts from the expectations he grew up with, late in life and in astounding ways. I appreciate his courage. We're all bumbling through the unknown together. At least I still get to wear the sexy nighties. Sometimes.)

All our arrangements are atypical: committed, intimate relationship notwithstanding, we have separate dwellings, for instance. This is for the purpose of basic sanity. I require a modicum of order and aesthetics to function; it seems to me quite reasonable. Zalman's requirement for this is far less. In the course of his creative output, daily routine and grinding the wheels, he spews forth more chaos than I could have imagined possible. And in the midst of the books and the papers and the crumbs and the redundant machinery and gadgets and batteries and religious paraphernalia and telephones and wires, he accomplishes far more than I do. This works for us, more or less, because we have no children of our own. I do spend time with his, and I love them; but I know I can always escape. Would I find creative solutions if I couldn't? Would I nag him to death? Would I drive them all crazy with unrealistic expectations? Or would I go crazy myself?

My dreams of womanhood never included not having children of my own. It is absolutely clear that Zalman's ten are truly enough for him. They are wonderful. They accept and welcome me. And yet . . . Sometimes I am asked if I have 'completely come to terms with that'. I don't know if I will 'completely' come to terms with that before menopause. I feel in my blood and bones that a woman's life-path, the one so many in my generation are busy escaping from can be one of the most highly potent spiritual paths. Not only, as Joseph Campbell points out, does it require setting aside one's own needs for the good of the family and therefore overcomes ego; but it also calls forth all creativity, all sensitivity, all delicacy, all talents and, eventually, wisdom and compassion. I am one of so many who feels at a loss for not having children of her own. I wonder whether I will find when I am old that I have not actually loved deeply enough, not experienced a 'real' bond, not felt the mysteries of my body's creativity. Will I regret that I have not continued my mother's exceptional genes into the world? Will I grieve when Zalman is gone that no living fruit of our loving still grows? When I am old, will anyone love me enough to take care of me if I am in need? All of this, all of this. And yet, my body doesn't leap in desire toward my partner when I see babies, as it did some years ago.

So I ask myself if there is another way to learn that woman's spirituality, the kind meant for in this world. I have no answer, only hints. Peggy Rubin quoted an older Native American woman friend of hers as saying that so many of us are not having children now because the world is in such urgent need of 'grandmother energy', with wisdom to see beyond the needs of our own families to the needs of the whole, that we are skipping the mothering stage. I do not know the answer, yet.

And what does our sexuality mean, divorced from having children? I sometimes feel wistful, because such an acknowledgement of love wants to create for itself, to bear fruit. But making love is so many things: laughter, warmth, surprise, delight, play, intimacy, deep contact, loving, transparency, discovery. It heals and makes whole, and it seduces us beyond the comfortable borders of safety. It comforts and provokes. It requires surrender and strength. Wherever it takes us, even through fear, I can go without fear, because of our fundamental commitment. In the delicious mystery of the dance which quickens our beings, it holds the richness of all paradox. I am at a loss to describe the essence of our decision to partner only each other, sexually. ('Monogamy' sounds so anthropological.) Of course there are all the obvious practical reasons, traditional, familial, medical. Then there are all the personal idiosyncracies. I look at him, say in winter, in the middle of undressing for a romantic interlude, and there he stands, in his undershirt with the ritual fringes, skullcap, knit leg-warmers, and I think, 'God, is he cute!' Of course, *he* calls the disheveled woman with the graying hair, round belly and ample rear beautiful. We're neither of us blind, so this must be true love. But these are not really *it*.

It is a kinesthetic experience, harder to describe: I have a feeling that all that energy must flow into one place, the relationship between us, if we want to receive its real gifts. The containment makes a deepening. And of course, when I enter such risky places, I need all that trust. I do experience sex (even such safe sex) as risky business. It is precisely and only *him* that I want there, within me, embracing me. I mean, I could get catapulted far out into the Great Wow, and maybe never come back! Then when my scattered cells/selves do re-collect, they are interspersed with particles of him. Thank God it is him, because I am no longer quite who I was; *post coitus*, I am a mutant. Surely this is one of the Sacred Paths. Hidden in such an irresistible drive is a Way Home. In my head I know that we are never really separate from God. When we make love, the reality of what this may mean begins to unfold in my flesh.

I once had a visit, just after we made love, from the *Malakh HaMavet*, the Angel of Death, who told me: 'People fear me because they expect to see my face only once, when I come to take them. But I have been with you at all the important moments – of making love and conceiving life, in the inspiration to create, in loss, in all the little deaths that make room for change and growth. I am there in ecstasy, and in the seed. Look at my face. I am your friend.'

This is true. There are times when our lifestyle seems to go from one crisis to the next; when Zalman and I seem to have lost deep contact, and our communications taste bitter and lack understanding; when the work just seems too hard, and I am tired; when I feel unappreciated or unseen, and recite to myself a sour litany of discontent. It is the presence of death that broadens my eye and restores the full view, shifting my complaints (maybe real enough) into their truer place and size within the whole rich picture. For me this is pretty graphic: Zalman is 67, may he live to be 120! I am 42. It is likely that I will spend many years without him. But it is equally true for all of us; we none of us know when we may receive the unexpected visit from the *Malakh HaMavet*. Zalman and I take care not to go to sleep in anger. I am learning from him to practise forgiveness. We don't let pride keep us from apologies, or from acknowledging, even grudgingly, in the midst of anger, that we love each other.

Judith Jamison, in her splendid eulogy for Alvin Ailey, said it well: 'Death teaches us that *all* things are precious.'

ZALMAN M. SCHACHTER-SHALOMI

You had to snare us with the issue and its importance! I, who have been married three times and am now with a fourth partner, feel the pressing need for making explicit some of the assumptions that make me look still again for a committed relationship and for finding its sacred sustenance.

I pray that the writing will not shatter the fragile-subtle web that is ours. What I say is tentative and a kind of affirmation of hope and love. It becomes dated the moment it is written. This form of writing invites idealizations that are far from the real multidimensional currents in my own awareness-feelings as I am in and by my self. How much more so in the intense dance of two individuals who each have their own body tides, feeling ebbs, family, business and friendship pulls and tugs within the vicissitudes served up by life. What may look positive and permanent in print is in reality a snapshot of a momentary groping in life.

When I give myself to a philosophical consideration of relationships and their duration, I come up with notions rooted in our understanding of the experience of generations of primitive humans existing in caves and tribes. What got imprinted, reinforced and maintained by biological strictures over the millennia got codified into our make up and socially installed into the mores of our day. With the shorter life spans of earlier periods in history, seven to 10 years is a long time.

My intuition based on the above considerations is that relationships are meant by nature to last about seven years and then decay. I believe that there is a cycle that produces the seven-year itch. Seven years allowed a child engendered in a relationship to grow up past the cub stage. After that time, the cement that kept the parents together weakened to allow for transformations to other configurations. The offspring moved on to learn more of what it needs by apprenticing with and helping other adults who would take care of it and show concern for its further education.

As I surmise this anthropologically and apply it to who we are today, I feel that it takes more than the naturally imbedded responses to make a relationship last longer than that. Even within the 'week' of years there are differences in the dynamics of change. The Kabbalist in me schematizes the first of the seven years as *Hessed*, Grace, a gift of the Cosmos in the form of the intensity of the attraction and the joys of the first discoveries. The second year – the year of *Geburah*, rigour and severity in this scheme – is given to testing limits and boundaries, to definitions of mine and yours, and to the disillusionment with the real not fully being the dreamed-of ideal. If we have managed to survive the second year we can hope that in the third year, that of *Tiferet*, beauty, presence and compassion, we become more caring with each other. In the fourth, that of *Netzah*, victory, duration, the year of the skillful means, we would learn to share effectively and to satisfy each other's needs while taking care of our own. Then in the fifth, the year of *Hod*, splendor, glory, we learn to enjoy each other with elegance and gallantry, with beauty and artistry in the art of relationship. In the sixth year, that of *Yesod*, foundation, we experience the depth of profound bonding of sexuality inherent in the committed union; and then, having made it to the seventh year, we have reached that of *Malkhut*, majesty and transformation, as well as crisis-opportunity. A new cycle with the same or another partner can begin. In this schema each year has its own needs and tasks, its own pitfalls and opportunities for deepening.

This holds for the first, 'milk and honey' octave of Hessed, Grace (Hessed of Hessed, Geburah of Hessed, Tiferet of Hessed, etc.). Then begins the more abrasive and harsher octave of Geburah (Hessed of Geburah, Geburah of Geburah, etc.) The second octave is a 'severe' one. People who make it through to the third octave, that of Tiferet, can count on a long-lasting and continuing relationship, and so through to the 50th anniversary, a true Jubilee.

To be appropriate to each phase of the evolving relationship requires awareness and communication, a persistence in staying clear with each other. The occasions of needing to disconnect from each other as we are hurt by those we love and who love us tend to make us opaque. We react with the outmoded strategies we used when we were in the bosom of our early family – and which did not work well even then – and become even more distant and opaque and want to hurt as we have been hurt. An untended relationship grows weeds. The stash of disappointment and resentment accumulates when unexamined. In the end we have a growing dysfunctionality eating away at the roots of trust and commitment.

When I serve as marrying minister I suggest to couples to renew their covenant every three to four years and update according to the changes in all the dimensions of their lives. Occasional karma clearing and work on the relationship is essential. Growth makes for the need to readjust according to the shifts in interpersonal dynamics.

Besides the tides of the relationship between two individuals there are also the tides of times when we are transformed and different perspectives emerge and new possibilities are tested. I believe that each time creates the relationships that fit that time and that now the time is for exclusive commitment.

The 1960s held the promises of the sexual revolution. We learned much during those days and nights of exuberant explorations. Those were the times when I believed that the open marriage – one that was primary, the main relationship, one in which we are mostly married to each other and left free and unjealous to be lovingly intimate with others – was the way to relate in the most sacred and committed way. People can and should negotiate any contract they wish, and we know that all you need is love to make it all work.

In the 1960s, 1970s and much of the early 1980s I was ideologically wedded to 'open' relating and defended that point of view with vigor. I was not swayed by traditional arguments and moralizing. AIDS and the lesser scourges of herpes, chlamydia and other venereal diseases made me change my mind. Somehow I saw that the 'virtues' of monogamy had the sanction of nature. I realized that my insistence on admitting all kinds of access to me without discrimination, by not rejecting the loving sexual advances of others or the ones that arose in myself, reduced my emotional 'immune response' and shattered my psychic shield. I confused relationships and tore down my own boundaries, causing myself and others more grief than I could live with. In my previous marriages it did not work. Kicking and screaming I gave up on that ideal of the 1960s.

I still feel some sorrow on an ethical–philosophical level that the nature of how we are in sexual relationship is such that multiple partnerships are difficult to maintain. I have since learned that there are other, non-genital forms of emotional, intellectual and, most significantly, spiritual intimacy that satisfy the urge to relate closely with another and that create less confusion and bitterness.

After my third marriage became untenable and dissolved, Eve and I met and began to work together. The deeper we shared our values and strivings, the more we felt we had here the possibility of a partnership. This notion – partner – means much to us. Tired of being the one who supported, maintained and kept growth going in a relationship, I very much wanted a sharing partner. I wanted both to be able to share delights and pleasures, and to share the place of having and giving support when energies wear thin. If I am moved by visions and ideals,

I want to be able to match mine to my partner's, and pull and push together to make the better world happen.

Eve and I discussed what we need in a relationship. Dedication and a sense of the sacred are important to both of us, so that we might live in the sight and the witness of God and with His/Her blessings. We are clear that at this time this also means a committed monogamous and exclusive relationship.

Our communities know us as a couple. We maintain separate homes and share days and nights when our time is right. I have obligations of work and children, as well as work habits and patterns that are not harmonious with Eve's. So for this time we have found the way that best supports us in loving each other.

I am bruised by the legal and financial ordeals of past marriages. Since we do not expect to have children, this makes a renewable relationship feasible. I cannot at this time see how I can make a permanent and rigid commitment that does not take into account the changes we are going through. At this time I cannot – do not want to – be 'legally' married. Yet our bond is firmer than any other I have ever had. We have a renewable commitment. It is not a forever bond, although it aspires to infinite continuity. So we make our relationship renewable for each period. We have renewed and adjusted our contract each year or half-year. I/we need room to renegotiate and readjust the shifting details of our relationship.

We are fortunate that we share in many dimensions. We often work together, we meditate and worship together, we look for similar values and struggle with compatible issues. We like how we both are as sexual and sensual, emotional, intellectual and spiritual beings. She likes my children and they like her; she keeps me sane in relation to them. When I need to face something that I am avoiding, she is an ally in keeping my eye on the bigger picture. The things I do for her I hope are reciprocal.

We respect each other. I respect Eve more than I have respected any female partner. (I definitely had a sexist streak in me that did not credit women with real understanding. This blind spot needed much work and is not yet altogether gone.)

Being committed to growth and personal development is the 'diamond cutting' phenomenon. It takes one hard diamond to shape and cut another. The hard and jagged edges of a person cannot be rounded by 'consolers' who seem 'soooo understanding'. It takes the hassles of being in the presence of an unrelenting and loving other to make one see the need to shape up.

Besides the hard-diamond phenomenon there is the wonderful, benign deepening that occurs in the ongoing communication with a 'beloved' over an enduring period of time. I feel I know Eve and am known by her at greater depth and height than ever before. There is the pleasure bond, the mutual collusion to give each other delight. There is the rising and abating of passion, the shared deep arousal and stirring of elemental urgings from all the couplings of human and animal ancestors that have produced us. There is a loyal, reassuring closeness that allows for risky flights of transcendental consciousness and dissolving into full emptiness. There is the prayer of the flesh for the healing and the peace of the whole and of individuals. There is a divine 'Presence', a Sabbath of delight and safe-at-home-ness with the beloved.

We feel that the spiritual dimension of our lives is as much grounded in the sacredness of our sexual celebrations and liturgies of loving as in celebrating religious liturgies and sharing spiritual practices. The mutual meditations shared in touch, smell and taste melt the borders of skin and ego into a unity in which God is also a party. The spiritual dimension is explicit in our work and communication and a *sine qua non* for our intimacy. Some of our best pillow talk takes us into the spiritual dimensions of our lives.

My sense of our agreement is that I will strive not to let myself become opaque to Eve. At times this is not comfortable. I hate hassles and want smooth harmony and agreement. But I have found that we interact better in the long run when I am straight in my communication. It honours the other and gives the data they need to check their own perceptions for correctness. Feeling jealousy also means sharing it.

I share my delight with her in the beauty of other women. She does the same with me. We tell each other what and who turns us on. Owning, possessing, is not the issue.

For me, betrayal is connected with communication, privacy, and respecting vulnerability. I recall with pain when another partner in anger at me broadcast to others my own deep inner struggles, which I had confided in her in moments of loving trust. I believe that skill and the goodwill needed to do the work of rebuilding trust are essential. It is difficult to do that without a loving ally – therapist, teacher, helper – a witness for both parties.

There are conflicts between our needs as individuals and our needs as a couple. For instance, when I am at my home and Eve is at hers, we feel less of a unit and more like individuals than when we are travelling together away from Philadelphia. On these journeys we are a unit, moving together through space and time, through tasks and delights. Then we are more 'we' than I and she.

The boundaries between public and private lives are fuzzy. The basis of my public persona is charisma and friendship, rather than professionalism. Eve is a private person; for her, the boundaries between her professional and personal lives are clear and in high contrast. This leads to some friction. I am learning to make some boundaries, and Eve is more accepting of my 'friends', just as they are more accepting of her at my side. At times I feel it comes down to scheduling, timing, and tact.

Crucial for our harmony is staying aware of the difference in our ages and the consequent tensions around the differing phases of life. I am 67 and she is 42. I am in grandparent phase (although I have a seven-year-old as my youngest child, who is the uncle of older nephews and nieces – the children of my oldest, who is 44) while Eve could now be in the 'empty nest' phase and have kids at college. So in this way I get the benefits of her youth: beauty, vigor and outlook, and she gets the benefits of my age: prominence, experience, and perspective.

To resolve issues between us we talk and share and see our therapist and do what we can to learn the dynamics of our interaction. We have some rules: we do not take up difficulties when in bed. When we need to sort things out we go into another room. We express our regrets and sorrow at having hurt the other and beg to be forgiven. Eve was first to apologize to me. I was not used to that. In past relationships I was the one who was in the doghouse. I was the one who had to offer the meek amends on the altar of 'family peace'. It healed something in me and made me offer my apology with humility, not humiliation. There is an explicit understanding that we do not want each other to be bent out of shape as the cost of our love.

Rereading what I've written it looks much easier than it is. When the tension is high I am beset with doubts as to whether we can or should make it together. At times we look to the angel who connects us with disdain and incredulity. Then she/he reminds us of the impermanence of our tension, the value of our presence to each other, and that this is just another screeching 'diamond cutting' time.

I cannot say which part of the whole is the essential thing that cements our life. Like the heart and the brain and the liver, each separate item is a vital organ, each as important to the whole scheme as the other. I delight in Eve's mind and soul, her vision and art. If we did not have a juicy sexual relationship, we could not endure. But the sexual alone would not do it either. The spiritual connections give us long-term goals; the sensual and aesthetic nourishes our working together; and the work in turn makes us appreciate the other parts. But most of all I do not hunt any more for the 'anima' who will juice me with her magic. I have found a partner, I love her, and as much as one can be in this, of all possible worlds, I am reasonably happy.

Finally, I want to say that, although I cannot chronicle all the shifts that have occurred in my outlook on our relationship, there is one that I need to spell out. It arose in my heart as a result of writing this, and it is that I no longer really think and feel as if Eve and I were in a terminable, *ad hoc,* renewable relationship. While the details of how, where and when might shift, my commitment to her as my enduring mate is firmly anchored in my heart. I feel that I am fiercely and zealously – jealously – committed to her in a love that belies my philosophizing. I am surprised by this and, as I said in the beginning, I pray that the spelling out in writing will not shatter the mighty, strong and yet fragile-subtle web that is ours . . .

PENELOPE SHUTTLE

Fruits, fruits only grow from a meeting of
opposites, male and female . . .[1]

Peter and I met on my first visit to Cornwall, in the summer
of 1969. It was a chance meeting. I was staying with friends
at Tregarthen, near Zennor in West Penwith, in the far west of
Cornwall, when Peter came over to discuss plans for the St Ives
Poetry Festival. West Penwith is high moorland: gorse; heather;
bracken; some cultivated tracts of land; rocky outcrops, ancient
stones, ever-changing shades and shadows of sea, sky and land.
I'd been living for some months in Somerset, having moved
from urban Middlesex, but this was more than countryside; this
was not England! It was a different land, having a profound
stillness of earth, of stone, and a glittering lurching light from
sea and sky; an enclave agitated yet peaceful, simmering yet
stable; changing and changing, a place of second and third and
fourth thoughts, on to infinity. The very names, the last living
traces of the lost Cornish language, were speaking their poetry.

In this strange beautiful magical and auspicious place, of
barrows, standing stones, cromlechs, carns, little fields, moors
and stone hedges, Peter and I met. We realized almost at once
that we shared the same reality. What do I mean by this? I mean
a threefold reality: of poetry; of love erotic, spiritual (and, later,
parental); and of Cornwall (not England), weather and
landscape and separateness. This reality seized us and we
seized it. Not the least powerful of the three strands of reality
is Cornwall. Cornwall has been the third sometimes obstrep-
erous theme in our relationship, gladly embraced because it
signified our beginning and our continuing life together,

sometimes resisted because of its contrariness, its weather and strong moods.

After this first meeting, where we could only speak briefly because of there being many other people around, we corresponded and exchanged books. We met a little later in Somerset where we spent three weeks of discovery and exhilaration together.

At this time I was writing novels and Peter only poetry. Through the contagiousness of love and writing-enthusiasm we exchanged hats as it were; over the next few years Peter embarked on his remarkable series of novels, beginning with *In the Country of the Skin*, [2] which sprang from the adventures of our first times together, and I returned to my first chosen form in writing, poetry; we were beginning to become one another.

And becoming one another we became more our ownselves, in this shared life of language and sex.

So Cornwall and writing brought us together. But we were also brought together by adversity and unhappiness. At this time I was struggling with the deep and paralysing depressions that later opened out into the dreams and the releasing work between us that led to the writing of *The Wise Wound*, [3] and new visions of writing for us both. Also when we met Peter was deep in the painful disintegration of his first marriage. So we were both at crisis point; and in need of healing. Soon we were living together in Falmouth. Being together all the time promoted mutual healing and renewal. I do not want to overstate matters, and when two people have come out of dark times there will be struggles and more pain; but the sense of arrival at a haven was very strong for us both. You see, we had both experienced the isolation writers suffer within family life. Writers live a writing life, and that life is a quest; it is hard to comprehend such a quest unless you are on it yourself; and almost impossible to convey it to someone not on that route. Both Peter and I had experienced 'the ancient enmity there is' [4] between creative work and everyday life. We both knew the struggle to get jobs that didn't destroy our writing energy; knew the need to get time and strength to do our writing work, knew how important and perilously difficult it is to protect the writing core. We knew the hunger of the writing. It bonded us then; as now. And because we share this reality of being writers, we can understand how difficult and joyful it is to write, to contemplate and transform and extend the experiences of life into poetry and through other writers. Perhaps no one but another writer can comprehend the blisses and torments of writing. And so from negation and frustration and unhappiness and isolation as writers we came to a new beginning; to negotiation with one another and our own creativity; working towards new ways of responding to the world; building up our new selves with the tools and confidences of our shared life.

Both of us were wounded, as who is not, by the strictures of over-masculinized society; of living by its wrong rhythms; and it was through work on patterns of feminine identity and body/spirit experiences that we drew closer together. Discovering and defining a new concern for the recovery of the female dynamic in society and the individual woman; an acknowledgement of what is owed to and needs championing in the still-silenced sex, woman; explorations of the riches to be found behind the taboos of the menstrual cycle, the despised body of the life-giving and life-bringing woman – all gave me an enormous release of personal selfhood, a great creative charge; and as Peter will say for himself, he too was released from long-held tensions and mysteries by our attention to this area; which he has pursued in the challenging and engrossing work *The Black Goddess;* which actively seeks to rediscover those predominantly female senses other than the visual/rational; those senses of touch, smell, weather, atmosphere, electro-magneticism, mistakenly seen as lesser; the senses we are homesick for; and the censoring of which wounds us all. *The Black Goddess* is a man's menstrual vision.

Intimacy then in our relationship pivots on three elements in our shared reality: poetry; sex; Cornwall. But how do two people write, man and woman, when they write both their collaborative works and their own works? Imagine it to be like the alchemical double pelican; one person reads the other one's work and absorbs it into themselves, like the child of the pelican feeding from the blood of the maternal breast; then, nourished by the work, that writer will write; and in turn offer that work back to the partner, offering the sustained breast on which the other may feed; this continues, this giving and taking of nourishment. We have always read each other's work in progress and used phrases and ideas freely from each other's work; they are freely given; they change as they go from one to the other; are absorbed and translated and woven into our own individual work, like a mutual shared tapestry, a banner carried forward between us. In some works, the collaborative works, the page will be shared between us; ideas and images flowing through; in the separate works, the other will be there like an invisible spirit animating the work. Thus we are contained one in the other; sharing the same reality; this is an alchemical interchange. (It does not rule out heated discussions on some points in our work!)

Like most poets (like most people) we are not grown-ups; when we began living together, released from two unhappy tense backgrounds, we were able to allow ourselves to be children together; by approaching again a lost innocence I think we were able in a sense to go back to the very beginning, and begin growing up together. In a relationship between man and woman there will always be, as well as two lovers, a brother and sister and a mother and a father. We went back to find gentler versions of those persons, and I hope have started some growing up without the conflicts that had riven us before we met. It was rescue on both sides.

To get a hold on your true self, your authentic self, you need a partner who is able to give, as well as him/herself, to give you your self. If I had to define what began love between Peter and I it was that for the first time in my life I was able to be myself; without pretence; defence; or fear; no mask; no disguise. Muriel Rukeyser asks: 'What would happen if one woman told the truth about her life?' And answers herself: 'The world would split open.'[5] But in our relationship 'telling the truth about myself', which is what poetry is about for us all, led not to the world splitting but to the world healing; it led to a working companionship and a way of living without hierarchy or denigration; our shared work is woven into our life and tells in its own words the way we live; flesh and spirit; one flesh; giving us both our individual strength; and freedom to be . . .

Poetry can remind us how extraordinary the ordinary is; that what we see as familiar is also present in a dimension of wonder. And poetry is a bodily experience; it comes from the oldest brain and the deepest tissue. And it floods into the sexual area. Marion Milner speaks of 'the body's astonishing capacity to leap totally out of itself in the orgasm into something dazzlingly different, a dazzling infinity.'[6] And so poetry leaps totally out of itself. In my poem, 'Act of Love',[7] I've spoken of this as 'the clairvoyance of orgasm'.

When you write, you try to tell the truth. Our relationship is monogamous because it is difficult to tell the truth otherwise. Lying is not a good training for poetry. The mutual illumination sex brings us is of a poetic nature. Everyone of us experiences this sometimes but perhaps not enough people concentrate on it and open the way for it to increase. Love-making, especially when it respects and follows the highs and lows of the woman's cycle, can become a Tantric experience. As we try to contain and repair the damage to the earthly environment then as lovers maybe we should be repairing the damage done to sex, by a raping culture, and consider how in our intimacy we can move towards the greening of the orgasm; so that its revelations are not lost but lovingly directed into the flow of our lives.

Act of Love

At night, riding our bed like a willing and dethroned horse
we are secret depositors proud of our flaws,
flaws that scratch a diamond;
you are a stinging mirror to me, I another to you.
We are each a bird ruthless as cat
but we let that cruelty go into the dark
and lie lithe as lizards, side by side,
our fingernails extracting silver from our hearts,
the distinctive lode we work,
darkness arcing with our buck and doe brights
until we rest for a little, partners slumped on the ropes of night's
    ring.

Our outstretched arms anchor us, inseparable;
my nipple is hard as diamond, treble and desirous;
my breast-skin soft as unchaperoned moss;
your hand on it a serious shimmer;
my breast grows newer, newer,
my yanked-open laceless nightgown's bodice,
its cotton seam is caught tight around my ribs
where my heart is beating gravely and loudly,
its blood full of Burmese strength and mystery.

The night outside is a teetotal drum we flood into silence
as your delicate hard sex presses against my hip;
when we meet and join we hold our breath,
then breathe out all the burning novelty of our bodies,
a big vapour furling into the room, flag
made from our clear-sky flesh, our unearthly diplomacy,
our hauntingly-real fuck;
I watch my familiar but elaborately-lifted leg
misty and incredulous in the straight-faced dark.

And as we are not blind or dumb
this is the time we stare and cry out best
as we wear out our weariness with thrusting,
our eyes open and glossy, our throats humble with aahs,
sighing into inaudibility, our lips soft reams
of silence; we're giddy with our tongues' work,
as if two serpents had become brother and sister . . .

As we cast ourselves into the night and the act,
our smooth knuckles shine,
we are gasping as we smell the sleep to come,
waiting for us beyond this untraceable room;
now we clamber the summit of old-friend mountain,
rising faster in our clamour,
swinging locked-together in our bell-apple nakedness,
in the double-pink hammock of the night
made of touch and breath,
(the purposes of the engineering!),
a labour of love as we rush towards that trembling edge,
toppling over yelling into the fall, the rapids,
the waters we enter, fluid as them,
my sex hot and hidden, perfect and full,
the corner of our sinews turned,
a clear answer found, its affirmative leaping from our mouths,
my body's soft freight shaking and accepting
in the clairvoyance of orgasm,
and your answering sheer plunge from mountaintop into river,
flowing where the bed was.

Sleep takes us then and drops us into its diocese,
drops us from night's peak into a dawn
of martial ardour, of trees mad
with old-clothes spite, a morning
where the starving still wait for us,
each with their lonely cloudy gaze.

So only the sugars of the night offer us any breakfast,
only our night's act of love feeds us,
the remembrance of our bodies like slow-moving turtles
lifted from the sweetness of a sea of honey,
flying into more sweetness.

Only the touchwood of our sweet bed
dams the savage sour torrent of the day.

In the morning we must say goodbye, not hello,
goodbye until the untouchable day has gone
and the night recalls us again to our study,
to our sweating gypsy-wagon sheets,
our navaho pillows and rich pastures,
the mintage of our wild skins.

'Damage done to sex by a raping culture . . .' Indeed yes. Too
many people are ignorant of the female sexual capacity, in which
the successive orgasms can reach spiritual-sexual levels, as in
Tantrism; and this goes with the ignorance of the female cycle,
the sensitive sexual and spiritual side of the menstruation which
has been tabooed by the patriarchal religions for so many
centuries. Robert Bly has declared that he is intent on repairing
the damage done to the male psyche by the patriarchy since
the beginning of the Industrial Revolution, less than 200 years
ago; he has also said that this damage has also been done to
the women, but over 2000 years or more. The knowledge that
I am proposing of the female cycle is exactly that knowledge
which was made taboo by the patriarchs, as any intent reader
of the Bible can see. It is now returning as a living capacity for
women; restoring this is like restoring the lost half of a severed
body.

What do Peter and I do? Well, you can see part of that from
my poem 'Act of Love'. If we can arrange our day in that way,
we love to spend at least two and a half hours making love,

continuing afterwards with our companionship in walking through the extraordinarily transformed ordinary landscapes around us and experiencing our direct continuity with nature and each other through skins which seem to have become transparent. That 'continuity with nature' is what I mean by 'greening the orgasm' and can only be adequately described in poetry, which is probably what poetry is for. Every thing becomes a most beautiful gift, the giving of which enables one to give back with the deepest life-forces found again in oneself. Sex in which my orgasmic potential has been realized, taking Peter with me to match the female capacity, becomes timeless, egoless, and natural. Peter has always practised yogic methods of controlling his ejaculation, so together we are able to make these explorations. My sexual fantasies are usually visions of places we have been together – they are visions more than fantasies that seem to arise through the skin – but that is usually as we begin and as we finish, other things that happen are indescribable, even in poetry, though they demand to be honoured in poetry. Peter's fantasies, like most men's, are somewhat darker, but we have room for those too. When I talk about 'championing in our own relationship' I mean that because of these experiences we seem to have to put each other first, because *we are each the other*, and because physically so, morally too, one flesh; though we also belong to Zoe, our daughter, who herself rose from these depths. Zoe is her own self, and our physical child; she is a sibling to a very large family of poems.

I suppose that it is a consequence of these intimacies and discoveries that we are so far – 20 years – seldom in serious conflict. During our first seven years together, we were far too interested in each other ever to exchange even a cross word. When I became a Mother (I will come to this again) adjustments had to be made and there were naturally times I had to choose between Peter and Zoe, so there were severe abrasions, but no bruises. Day 20 of my menstrual cycle can be a recurrent dangerous time as there is happening within me the racing change from things ovulatory to things menstrual and this is a conflict we can project and re-project on each other, though we usually manage to tumble over the threshold fairly amicably. We both keep a menstrual diary we have invented – called the 'menstrual mandala' – so we can keep track of any such days. Day 20 is usually a low time for me sexually and if I am a little tired it's one of the few times in the cycle I can't come, and this is inclined to make me fierce. It is clearly very important for women to know about these days. I may have a good transition dream of the rite of passage over this threshold – I was once helped across it by St Michael! – and then day 20 is no problem. We have kept records of our dreams ever since we met, and this enables us to reconstruct these rites of passage as well as seeing something of the way the cycle interacts with the environment, weather and season and so forth.

I was going to say that we like all-night sex too, that is to say, making love when we go to bed at night, and staying *in situ* to exchange electricities (using the 'scissors' position) until the morning, moving in and out of dreams back to a consciousness of our two selves joined, and into dreams again.

Of course there are on-going difficulties in living together; a flipside; nigredo; depressions; fatigue; misery; insomnia; all these difficult things return. But to work through these times we try to remember how such dark times have been experienced before and survived. Look into the mirror of the shared years and trust what will happen again; that one of you will be able to stay steady at the helm through rough seas; take it turn by turn. I think the most difficult time for us was when our daughter was born; no matter how you work at it, there is baby shock. You both change. When a woman is pregnant she is two people at once, and her partner has to relate to her in new ways on top of the old ones, or even let them go for a time. During my pregnancy (now 15 years ago) I wrote comparatively little; but Peter amassed a huge amount of poetry-in-draft which became his book *The Weddings at Nether Powers;*[8] it was as if during my pregnancy he too had been pregnant with this wondrous poetry, and during the years of baby shock this was his lifeline, the sign that our life together as poets was merely in temporary eclipse, as indeed it has proved, for now we are working more closely than ever, the more closely because of the few years when we had to reallocate our energies to our new roles. When our daughter was born we'd been living together seven years. We married when she was three years old. This was severely practical, and intended to ensure we could control and protect each other's literary estate!

Having a child is, as we soon find out, sorrow and joy, loss and gain, sacrifice and reward. The way any couple brings in the third, the child, is their own; infinitely complex, personal, difficult and thrilling; every adaptation is their own, unrepeated by any other couple, unrepeatable; the redefinings that have come from it have deepened my way for me; and for Peter, I think, the role of father, spoilt by his own childhood and by a too early first marriage, has been redeemed, simply by being understated, freer, more open. Poets have so many children of the word, the spirit, that they strongly need the human child; but there are the conflicting demands, it can't be otherwise. . . . Where does a child fit in to the three-stranded shared reality; she is part of all three. And yet still 'poetry was where I lived as no one's mother, where I existed as myself.'[9] But Peter is with me.

References

1   Marion Milner, *Eternity's Sunrise* (Virago Press, 1987).

2   Peter Redgrove, *In the Country of the Skin* (Routledge & Kegan Paul, 1973).

3   Penelope Shuttle and Peter Redgrove, *The Wise Wound* (Grafton Books, 1986).

4   Rilke, in his letters.

5   Muriel Rukeyser, *'Kathe Kollwitz'* (Pocket Books, 1973).

6   Marion Milner, *Eternity's Sunrise* (Virago Press, 1987).

7   Penelope Shuttle, *The Lion From Rio* (OUP, 1986).

8   Peter Redgrove, *The Weddings at Nether Powers* (Routledge & Kegan Paul, 1979).

9   Adrienne Rich, *Of Woman Born* (Virago Press, 1977).

PETER REDGROVE

There was this young woman over by the window in the house at Zennor. She was reading a book, but not as I had seen others reading books. There was a quality of attention, of *listening* as she read, as though the book was all that was visible of another person, whom she could see entire. I learnt that this was Penelope Shuttle, and that she was a novelist. One of her books was on the table.[1] I opened it and read. I had seen nothing like it before: it was the story of three people in a sexual triangle and though they were almost entirely caught up in their jealousies they moved through a clairvoyant world that sparkled and hummed with awareness that the characters only intermittently shared. As in Wallace Stevens, they were unhappy people in a happy world. Shuttle's sentences slid over each other, chatoyant, exposing layers of texture, sound, scent, abrasion, silkiness, sentences of every kind that explored the spaces they created like fighting ants and bejewelled leopards establishing domiciles. I was reminded of Rimbaud, extended. I have since heard celebrated by the French feminists of the 1980s 'the feminine sentence' and the quality of *jouissance* in writing, and the notion that language may be as much a vital plasm as a personality is, and that writing is the plasm of the world, and the two may interact to find a transcendent completion. This was in summer, 1969. I also learnt from Shuttle's blurb that she had 'itinerant boyfriends', and lived in Frome, near Bristol. I tucked this useful item of information away.

My first marriage was in disarray. I had fled to Ireland, where I sought oblivion in the dark and velvety world of Dublin and Guinness, in and on which I lived for three weeks. My turds resembled the graphite of pencils. A kind lady put me on the plane to Bristol. It was time to renew my acquaintance with the novelist Shuttle. I rang, and agreed to meet in the George, at Frome. Her mother (who lived far away) had remarkable skills as a dressmaker, and Shuttle stepped into my life with a wardrobe full of 'the long series of wonder-awakening dresses' which were the sartorial equivalent of the feminine sentences the daughter constructed: 'her wonder-awakening dresses, star-rays combed into a shaggy dress, bone-flounce skirt, turbinal blouse . . .' – quite an eyeful. I could not wear the dresses, but I could do my best to allow the feminine sentence to write through me, and for a while I became the novelist, and she the poet. My first novel was called *In the Country of the Skin* and it was a record of the passionate multi-media show of our first months of living together, and it was not a patch on Shuttle's work. Two sentences in a piece of her work in progress had altered me and brought me through to my own novel: 'In the distance I see a bridge of white granite. Whistling its tune, night ends . . .'[2]

During those first months together the personal equivalent of the dark rhythms of the prose books manifested itself in intense depressions late in Shuttle's menstrual cycle with intense cramps when the period came. The atmosphere at these times crackled with unaccountable electricities and screaming nightmares. I had studied analytical psychology and dream analysis for many years and had recently spent some 18 months as a pupil of Dr John Layard, who himself had studied with Homer Lane, C.G. Jung and had published many seminal contributions to psychology and anthropology. With the help of Layard's methods I helped Shuttle draw a picture of the depressions – she could not write them – and then to dream vividly as a consequence. She dreamed every night for five months, and we analysed the dreams every day, in sessions often lasting many hours. There was great concern at one point when some astronauts appeared with their machine and penetrated an eye-like Earth right through its axis – this was a 'great dream' which portended either disaster like a brain tumour or a penetration to new levels. When she woke, Shuttle had begun a series of intense headaches. When she went to the opthalmologist he looked at her heavy spectacles after his examination and said 'You don't need these.' So the dream was a healing dream after all. With the dreams so vividly and physically present, the premenstrual time now became intensely creative and the cramping bleeding uncramped itself and became an extraordinary vagina-time. Her vagina is the one thing we did not share with our daughter, as medical technology resulted in a caesarian. That was seven years ahead.

We did not look up any books on menstrual psychology as we did not want to pre-empt the dream story that was unfolding round the cycle of descent and return, of the restoration of the Goddess Persephone, the Fallen Daughter. Eventually, though, it seemed sensible to seek illumination from other people's work and advisable to consult the literature. There must be a lot, we thought, as 50 per cent of the human world menstruates. WE FOUND THAT THERE WERE NO BOOKS ON THIS SUBJECT. This is why we wrote *The Wise Wound*, [3] and published it in 1978, since when it has remained in print.

Horasis was centrally important to us. This is Barbara Walker's word for mutual illumination during sex. As everybody knows, sex can take you to the deepest creative depths, and its energy can enthuse with their actual natures person and world. Two things stand in its way: one is when the man will not train himself to withhold his ejaculation long enough for the woman to expound her whole orgasmic capacity; the other is when the menstrual cycle is not sufficiently studied by the woman to find those days which are best for sex – orgasmic windows, you might call them, in the cycle. It is also the best thing to choose a position – such as the 'scissors' – in which one can not only make love effectively in mounting peaks but, without uncoupling, relish the deep relaxation moving into dreams and out again to waking. Games of all sorts can be welcomed as aspects of this *jouissance*, part of the novel.

Let me respond to some of your direct questions. We were perfectly happy unmarried, until we discovered that you can't put half a house in another's name without being mulcted of taxes, nor has a common law partner any rights or control over their partner's estate, nor has the partner's child any. I couldn't bear the thought of the way the law could victimize either of us if anything happened to the other, so we agreed to get married. Of course we were already married and sacramentally too in an alchymical wedding; or, to put it another way, John Layard maintained that the illegitimate relationship was the strong one.

In sexual alchemy – which is to say an artists' relationship that is erotic – you cannot hop from partner to sexual partner. The Work is a long process, and the Soror and Frater Alchymica work on each other and the work works on them for as long as it takes, which may be a lifetime. When you make love with a person, you interchange essences. This is why promiscuity fragments; now AIDS seems to reinforce this message. Concentration is needed, an accustomed temenos or laboratory, Minnebett or esplumeor charged with these conscious essences that distil and redistil, as Penelope has described in speaking about the Double Pelican. One life must be as open as that to the other, and only then do the partners symbolize the universe to one another. This must not be mistaken for current ideas of 'romantic love'. It is hard chemistry.

No man seems to understand this first principle: when the

child arrives the lover is no longer the lover, the child has become the lover. This is nature's provision and there is a set of female instincts that puts the child at the centre, for otherwise it might not be adequately cared for. In my first marriage I felt betrayed by the relationship so radically altering – nobody teaches men that this will inevitably occur. It is why so many men start affairs just at the time when the lover should have changed at least temporarily into the father, as the nest needs protection. I was guilty of ignorance. Which didn't make it much easier when our daughter arrived in my second marriage, but it did prevent me blowing it, and I gave what I could, even though it sometimes seemed to me that I had lost the best thing in the world, our alchymical work. Which, as it happened, we hadn't.

Better than 'romantic' . . . It is best to say that we live a 'poetic' life together and as we are freelance writers this also means hard graft, as the first thing that suffers in a recession is trifles like authorship. I say this in response to your query about whether the individual sense of purpose or destiny conflicts with our relationship. All our writing is so closely shared and formed between us that there is not (so far in 20 years and some 30 books written together) this conflict. Love-making often leads to a creative clarity, and creative work often leads to a deeper love-making; we both rejoice in each other's small worldly successes though I cannot say what would happen if either one of us became lop-sidedly successful; I think in that event one must take the money and run and hide, for the media pull people's images about in distorted ways. We are happy if we can make a living within which we can continue the Work. I think I have moved further towards the feminine than Penelope has towards the masculine; this is because society is ill-balanced towards the latter.

Undoubtedly our work on menstruation together formed the deepest of bonds. During our study of Penelope's dreams and my own, it would often happen in the early months that I bled (from my anus) on the morning of the day when her period was due. This was the outer sign of a deep mental resonance, which has persisted. I will almost every month experience the distress of the late luteal phase (about day 20, when the corpus luteum in the ovary is working at its peak, yet the egg itself if not impregnated is breaking up) at the same time as Penelope, and many of its physical troubles, especially in the skin. I dream at this time, or she does, the dreams of the great paradox of the female cycle: that the death of a potential child brings spiritual renewal by its sacrifice when the blood comes: one of the world's great tragic themes, now restored to us in its actuality of the feminine after centuries of taboo. This renewal happens for both of us, and is accompanied with an especial sexual high, which is alchemical and transforms the perceptions, so that everything that falsely appeared dull and 'ordinary' is transformed to the extra-ordinary, and makes poems that testify to the joy and strangeness of descent and return. In sharing her cycle I have moved towards the feminine: 'I found God in myself and I loved her fiercly' (Ntozake Shange).

Of course I have blotted my copybook irretrievably red for danger by collaborating in a book on menstruation, and have received many insults from the masculinist establishment as a result. In France this would not happen, as feminism is advanced there sufficiently to include sexual man into feminine gender, and physical, body transforming *jouissance* into poetry. (I have been scorned by several reviewers for writing as though suffused with 'the beatific vision' when I have simply been describing what the language allows me to say of what sex shows me; just as Penelope's superb erotic poem 'Act of Love' in *The Lion From Rio* has been called 'a brave effort' as though she were not describing actualities.) But, as they say, 'No sex, please, we're British.' I expect the literati will learn to fake their orgasms as we move culturally into Europe.

I am far from being a perfect lover, even though I am 60. I have many hang-ups. I have been very lucky. The first time

I had adult sex with a woman, my first real poem slid into my head. My mother on the other hand was an unhappy and imaginative woman who confided in me distresses that I now know are inflicted by patriarchy. I took harm from my parents' deeply divided marriage, and good where it might be least expected. I suppose I was 10 when my mother would still take me in bed in the mornings for a cuddle. The deep pulse that came from her body and filled the bed like wings beating was her femininity and caring and the natural bliss of her body, and I suppose you could also call it non-genital karezza. To know this once and to find it again more than once with other women, this subtle carnal spirit, is a singular fortune, and gives one faith in sex. I tried to describe its importance in my *The Black Goddess*, which says it is what people call the Holy Spirit, and the wings were those of the Doves of Ishtar.[4]

Wolfgang Lederer wrote about this in his *The Fear of Women*.

> 'Any love, after that first one, is, after all, at least a partial transference; and thus with any woman whom we love we commit incest by proxy. In last analysis, our actual mother was, herself, only a stand-in – a proxy for nature, for the mother-archetype, for the Unconscious, for the whole dark realm of the emotions, for the Goddess – put it any way you will. Through her, as by a bridge, or a pipeline, or a navel cord, we are in touch [with reality].[5]

Yes, all very well, if you are 'in her touch' you are in the thing itself. Sexuality is one of our great spiritual resources. The trouble is that we have borrowed most of our guiding models of spiritual experience from the patriarchy. I believe Freud is usually right about men: you should have seen the instinctual fury on my father's face as he brought in the tea and saw in his 10-year-old son's face the glow of carnal understanding. 'Get out of there my lad,' he rasped, 'get out of there.' And I got – but on wings.

References

1   Penelope Shuttle, *All the Usual Hours of Sleeping* (Marion Boyars, 1969).

2   Penelope Shuttle, *Rainsplitter in the Zodiac Garden* (Marion Boyars, 1977).

3   Penelope Shuttle and Peter Redgrove, *The Wise Wound* (Grafton, 1986).

4   Peter Redgrove, *The Black Goddess* (Grafton, 1989).

5   Wolfgang Lederer, *The Fear of Women* (Harvest, 1968) p.232.

Frances & Christopher Greatorex

FRANCES GREATOREX

I am reminded of something that I said to a friend on having just met Christopher – that I had met the person I would like to spend the rest of my life with. Although it was said in a somewhat unromantic, matter-of-fact, sort of way, the force that lay behind this statement led me to pursue him unashamedly until he got the message! Such was the strength of purpose that lay behind what I now consider to be my very deep-seated choice of soul playmate, that I believe it has been a vital component in us arriving at this point, 25 years on, still choosing to continue on our paths together.

I was attracted by the beauty and apparent strength in Christopher from the first time we met, and that beauty and strength has grown. It was, however, fairly soon into our marriage that I realized, to my dismay, that he had very little sense of the beauty or strength that I saw within him. This shook me profoundly, for I carried little sense of my own self-worth and therefore had much investment in him standing strong in the world beside me. The tentative trust that was beginning to build in myself began to be shaken and left me feeling horribly let down, confused and alone.

I responded to this predicament by taking on the cause of proving Christopher wrong come what may, needing desperately to convince him of those qualities that he carried within him but denied. Thus I found myself quite readily turning my full attention and giving priority to this cause, seemingly turning away continually from pursuing my own career as a painter. It often felt like a betrayal of my own process, and indeed many times I felt pulled in two. Looking more closely, I now see that, paradoxically, taking on this supportive role was indeed the necessary step on my path towards learning to give support to myself, that is by first learning to give to another. Ironically enough, a short time later, Christopher became so seriously ill and dependent on me that I was to be given the perfect opportunity to fully act out this supportive role.

By the time I met Christopher I had already survived and extracted myself from a dismal two years' marriage and various subsequent affairs that had done nothing to strengthen my self-image, so on looking back I find it quite extraordinary how, coming from such experiences, I could so readily, and so soon, plunge headlong into another committed relationship, which I did the moment I met him.

At the time of our meeting I had been accepted into art college in London. This was the first major choice I had made for myself in my life, and so, although somewhat timidly, I was out in the world fresh, feeling a new sense of excitement and freedom in taking charge of my life, and ready to pursue my career as a painter. It turned out that Christopher lived conveniently close to my college and so in very little time I moved in with him. And here my conflict began. I soon became totally absorbed by our relationship, and was ultimately so exhausted by the seemingly continuous need to choose between my work and relationship that I left college early and retired to a nice little cottage in the country with a lovely big dog, two cats and with Christopher home most Sundays. There was to follow the most awful first few years of married life, where we found ourselves victims of a system in which we were caught and by which we were diminished, which contained hidden promises, expectations and assumptions that were part and parcel of the unconscious marriage contract that we had taken on quite unquestioningly. I became frequently physically ill and twice ended up in hospital, and I survived this period by continually breaking down and being depressed, which took up most of my time and energy. Sometimes I negotiated these crises with professional assistance, but mostly alone.

Christopher took refuge within another relationship at the work situation that he hated. Although this affair lasted two years and it took much longer to rebuild the tentative trust between us, ironically it was my discovery of this infidelity that shook us out of our depressing stupor. It was quite clear we were in a mess. I suggested very seriously that in order to remain friends we should get divorced and continue unmarried.

This was an early indication of my growing disappointment in marriage as I knew it, and also of my need to express and experience friendship – something I had had very little experience of. We did not act on this suggestion, but it created considerable energy out of which we chose consciously to start afresh, take more charge of our lives and start a family. This was when my supportive role started in earnest.

We brought to our marriage many unaddressed childhood wounds and thus considerable fear about being out in the world at large. Early on in our relationship I was asked, quite unexpectedly, why I had married. 'As a safe place to grow,' was my hasty reply. Safe is hardly the word I would use to describe the majority of our life together, but safe enough it clearly has been, and grow we most certainly have. For we have discovered our roots in quarrying into the depths of ourselves to find the strength needed to meet the challenges that we have been given.

We discovered early on that, between us, we have a considerable ability to create a beautiful and nurturing environment around us, where to a large degree we have found the nourishment we needed for ourselves, our family and others. This was expressed particularly in the first years of child growing, when we built and ran a beautiful country restaurant and smallholding, which looked from the outside a haven of peace and tranquillity and everyone's idea of the perfect dream come true. This did for some time seem to give us the safety and protection that we thought we needed from the harsh outside world, but the inevitable limitations of the closed system that we had created for ourselves made us frustrated, and maintaining this dream-like reality ultimately became impossible as we began to connect to our more individual needs to break out and grow. The very same safe haven had become a cage.

Ironically it was Christopher becoming seriously ill with cancer that gave us the push we needed to break out, and the challenge we needed to turn much more of our attention from our outer environment to the environment within ourselves, something we have continually done since.

He was cured by harsh allopathic methods which left him a hollow shell, and it has taken years of complementary medicine and therapy, along with the growing love and trust for himself and between us, to heal the wounds, to allow him to stand strong in the world and to render him now very able to give help and support to others in need. All the stored up fury of his primal and childhood neglect was unleashed through the cancer and we were ill equipped to contain it. Any sense of safety that we had created seemed lost to us. The doubts and fears and feelings of inadequacy that we both carried about ourselves became energized perhaps because of meeting our impotence in the face of such a situation. Such was the darkness that engulfed us at times that it often became a fight for personal survival on all levels. We met, during those struggles, the most destructive parts of ourselves and yet, thank God, the most beautiful too. Both polarities became highlighted by the intensity of the enforced intimacy that we found ourselves in, as Christopher became completely dependent on me for many months. For along with the obvious emotional and psycho-logical stress, he also suffered the physical disability of damage to the peripheral nerves, which lasted for over two years. Neither he nor I brought much experience of intimacy to our relationship. I had been abused in my first two-year marriage, which left me feeling somewhat sexually inadequate and confused. So we brought both a lot of fear for, and yet a deep yearning for this intimacy. It has taken many years of patience and love to build enough trust for us to experience the intimacy that we now enjoy.

From our childhood experiences of not being seen or heard, inevitably comes our inability to see and hear. This tragic condition, I feel, has been at the root of most of the distress between us. For in not realizing the origins, nor yet having explored the nature of this primal neglect, we often found our deepest feelings, those of having been profoundly wronged, being energized and brought to the suface more intensely than ever during Christopher's illness and subsequent treatment. In our inadequacy to cope with such deep and passionate feelings, and having nowhere else to put them, we often found ourselves turning ferociously against each other. We would become overwhelmed by the mistrust and fury that was being evoked between us, thus deepening the pain of no longer being able to communicate with each other. These moments often became a question of fight or flight.

Being the hard-nuts that we are, flight was not the usual route we took, so fight we often did, and at those times we could become a danger to ourselves and each other. These became cutting-edge moments between us, of the greatest inner challenge for me, and were often times of transformation. Sometimes, to meet the fearfulness of the moment, I was left with nothing to do but pray, and in those instances I experienced quite miraculously the fear draining right through me and being replaced by an overwhelming sense of peace and love. Somehow, as if by a distant whisper, I was reminded of my original choice, and that gave me the courage and the desire to continue come what may. I was then fairly unaware of that place within me from where that distant call had come, but as time passed it grew stronger and so did I, and I have begun to trust above all that place within.

There were moments though, when, by the very weight of our situation, we became depleted of strength and courage to continue together, and at those times we found solace and support from dear friends. These relationships, at times quite intimate, were God-given moments of respite from a situation that was draining us dry. In spite of the added hurt that these infidelities evoked within us, mostly we sensed that they were not against our relationship, as they actually gave us back some degree of lost identity and self-worth, and a brief moment of much needed breathing-space for and from our relationship. Paradoxically, we were then more able to rejoin each other feeling stronger, more loving, with a new sense of hope and trust in ourselves and for each other, and with a renewed will to go on. And all the time, as a sense of a deepening trust and friendship grew between us, so did my desire to continue the journey with Christopher grow stronger.

Even during the time of our affairs, we would share with considerable sadness our mutual desire for them not to be necessary. Their presence was an expression to us of a lack within our relationship which created a feeling in us both that we were living a sort of second-best situation. These feelings would energize our desire to work on ourselves more, and so ironically their presence kept us in touch with the growing deeper commitment that we were feeling towards each other as partners. Gradually, as time passed, the need of affairs diminished and it must be at least eight years since I had my second affair with a man who remains a dear friend to us both.

There is no way that the dramatic nature of much of our life together has not deeply affected our children Tim, now 19, Bruno, 17, and Sophie, 16. I feel pretty certain that so much attention taken from, and needed for, a parent or parents, inevitably leads to the children suffering some degree of neglect. Certainly that was the case for both Christopher and myself as children, and out of that experience we both brought to our marriage a strong desire for sense of family. It has been from our children, within our life as family, that our greatest shared source of delight and surprise has come. They have taught me, and are still teaching me, how to see and listen more. I believe and hope that they are now too experiencing more being seen and heard. I am aware of, and feel considerable sorrow for, the past neglect that they have experienced during the very vulnerable time of their growth, when I was torn between giving them what they needed and giving Christopher my full attention. I know that they are working with the consequences of that period of neglect as a part of their life processes. For my part, I have recently found healing in opening fully to the grief of the conflict caused within me at that time of crisis. Indeed, it was soon after the birth of Sophie that I had my gall-bladder removed. Interestingly enough, the Chinese call that organ 'The Decision Maker'. Mine had clearly been working overtime, as the stress of producing 15 stones, which had to be removed, resulted in it collapsing and becoming useless.

Clearly the trauma of that time has affected us all, and particularly the children. I do, however, take some comfort from the knowledge that they have shared the great delights of our times together too. Since neither Christopher nor I had ever experienced being a delight or an enjoyment to our parents, discovering this new and wondrous sensation with our children has not only been an obvious benefit to their health and healing, but has also most surely contributed towards the experience and expression of intimacy between Christopher and me. I do believe that being enjoyed is a vital contribution towards one's own health and most certainly plays a very important role within an alive and growing relationship.

A vital part of my nature is being a painter. Being a mother and painter all at once, not to mention everything else, has at times felt almost impossible. Yet I now see that striving to be so, whilst obtaining and maintaining some semblance of peace and harmony, has been the biggest challenge on the path towards my becoming whole.

Among other reasons, I paint to see myself. I have therefore in the past invested a great deal of myself in my work. Feeling more effective in this area of my life than any other has led me at times to exaggerate its importance, to the extent that it created such an imbalance within me that it continually led to a breakdown in my health. This in turn energized the need to readdress the balance by giving more attention to the nurturing part of my nature, which I was very out of touch with. I owe so much to Christopher, who has a strong nurturing aspect to his nature, and has given me so much patience and support, above all during my early years of mothering when I needed to paint as well. We have always been able to affirm each other in our roles as mother and father, and I have found enormous delight, and still do, in seeing Christopher together with the children. I think that this has redeemed something for me from my fatherless childhood.

Motherhood has been a sacrifice for me. Once again, it has been precisely in this sacrificing that I have found within me an ability to give, quite unknown to me before. As my need of role playing decreases – the children are growing away, and we are all growing up – I am needing to rediscover who else I am. This is requiring that I give to myself the same quality of attention that I have learnt through giving to my family. It makes me glad to think of motherhood as a possible training ground for us to learn about a quality and depth of giving that we can give back to ourselves (as well as to everything else we do), at the time of separation when we need it most. It gives a new dimension and meaning to all those years of child-growing. I am finding myself now right in the process of separation – moving from mother to friend. I am experiencing this as yet another level of maturing. Although it has been a vital aspect of growth within my relationship with Christopher – that is, shifting from dependence to independence and thus opening to the possibility of being friends and interdependent – I have had no early models of real friendship, and now with the children it is really stretching me to my fullest.

Over the years with Christopher, as we have individually grown stronger, so too has our relationship flourished. Since we now choose to receive support for our personal growth from therapeutic and personal relationships outside our own, our relationship is enjoying a new freedom and feels lighter and more able to express and become what it may be. It has moved through various stages. It has been a very closed and unconscious, yet safe sort of marriage, which contained and maintained us and our children quite adequately for some time, until, as the growing individuals we are, we began to feel restrained by such an isolated system. We then found ourselves breaking out into a most uncomfortable and essentially reactionary phase of individuation, where nothing felt safe any more, least of all our marriage, and where at times all seemed lost between us. Then I entered a phase when everything that I had thought, felt and experienced up until that point became questionable, and so did my relationship to everything and everyone. I met within myself, during that recent breakdown, an emptiness and aloneness quite unknown to me before, and nothing has had the same meaning since.

Recently I have, metaphorically speaking, leapt over and landed on the other side of a huge, high prison wall, and I now find myself free at last of the ties of my past. From here I see my numerous breakdowns as preparation for this breakthrough, and my marriage has been the springboard for this ultimate jump to freedom. Negotiating this major step on my path contained the risk of finding myself on my own, and the fear of this had been holding me back for some time. Realizing this, and with professional help, I took what felt like a hair-raising plunge into the unknown. To my considerable surprise, with some humour and huge delight, I met Christopher on the other side, still there!

It doesn't matter to me now whether or not I'm married to Christopher, and there doesn't seem to be any pressing reason to get unmarried, so little does this seem to have to do with my commitment to our relationship. Now we are entering a new stage of relationship where, for me, safety comes from my deep feeling of commitment to my journey ahead, and to travelling that path of uncertainty with him.

At times I have been tempted and seduced into believing that somewhere else, by doing something else, with someone else, I might find an easier and more enlightening route to God knows where! But I see now how 'hanging in there', attending to family matters and our relationship, has given me all the challenges needed to direct me back to attending to myself. Family and relationship has been my spiritual path. I am not sure about enlightenment, but I am very sure of the growing sensation within me of becoming much lighter – mostly lighter of fear.

Since my time of mothering is drawing to a close, painting is becoming my main activity and I know it will grow to be more and more so, but my relationship to it has changed. These past many years of maturing have been preparation for the task I now take on whole-heartedly as a painter. My growing fascination with colour and light is drawing me into quite remarkable areas as yet unexplored, and through my painting I hope to share these revelations with others. I know now that striving to do so is what above all else lies ahead for me.

Somewhere as children, like so many others, Christopher and I lost the ability to play and fear crept in. Through my experience of becoming lighter I am rediscovering a playfulness within me, and with this I am also becoming aware of a far deeper sense of the holy game that I am participating in. I am finding that I am embarking on a fascinating and enriching journey with other playmates where we are opening to our ability to be in a new sort of friendship or fellowship with ourselves, each other and the Divine, in which we play the game of life, where we welcome, indeed encourage challenging shots from each other, in order to discover the more our full potential. This is the lighter, freer and more playful quality of life that I am now enjoying and want to continue to participate in with Christopher. If we have reached half-time in our game together, then I feel that we have the best half to come.

CHRISTOPHER GREATOREX

Once upon a time I was asked by my therapist what my marriage was about and, without thinking, I said TRUTH. As we had just come through a particularly bad time, perhaps one of two occasions when we seriously contemplated divorce, this came as a bit of a surprise; but in thinking about it since, it occurs to me that no relationship can survive and grow unless it goes to the brink once or twice, or even from time to time.

Truth is such an abstract word. I suppose that what it means to me is to do with revealing the mystery in life and in particular through relationship with another. What I know is that it is through my relationship with a particular other that I have learnt more about myself, woman and relationship itself, than I have through any other area in my life. The woman is Frances.

It was not love at first sight, but it was intrigue. In all my previous relationships with women I had never contemplated marriage or life partnership. This one was different. Here was a mystery that went deeper than I had yet imagined and seemed to touch something in me about which I knew nothing but only sensed. This must be one thing that brings people together – a kind of longing, the drive for intimacy and self-knowledge. Much is often in the way of this fulfilment, and I think Frances and I both have wounds of childhood which have not only got in the way of intimacy but actually fuelled the fear of intimacy itself.

The principal dynamics seem simple and clear at this stage of our relationship. When I met Frances, 25 years ago, we lived together for two years before marrying. I was not wholly committed to the relationship, associating intimacy with devouring and wanting to keep my options open in case the going got tough. Part of my unconscious agenda within the marriage was to receive from Frances the nurture that my mother had never given me, and also the father guidance I had never received. Frances' side of the dynamic was similarly to receive from me both the attention and validation from a father who was unavailable to her, and also the nurturing of a mother. In both of our childhood experiences, there had been a way in which both parents had been missing. These are the kind of expectations on which many partnerships founder. Any lack in these expectations being met led to hurt and disappointment and a renewal of the childhood wound.

These projections and the patterns of behaviour around them often led us into fights until one of us, usually Frances, went to her pain, her woundedness, and intimacy was possible. This, however, was a kind of intimacy by default, obtained only by emotional catharsis. Not a lot of fun. Yet these fights were very important. Underlying both our issues were two people crying out to be seen. The difficulty was that we had built sophisticated defences to avoid being seen, especially if there seemed to be a demand for attention from the other. The inner demand to be seen and heard becomes so strong that the only way to get it met is to attack and break down the defences. The real problem is that this too can develop into a pattern which becomes more and more destructive.

It was around our 10th wedding anniversary (not something we have ever really celebrated) that I began to realize I was ill. If anything, I was the more damaged of the two of us in childhood and I would say that this came home to roost when cancer was diagnosed in 1978. This was a catalyst in our relationship. For six months I was completely dependent and Frances met the challenge, as she meets all challenges, head on. Despite the fact that our children were 3, 5 and 6, and needing their own care, she cared for me in a way which I had never experienced and met my childhood need. This began a kind of bonding and attachment that I had skilfully, albeit unconsciously, avoided till then. This in turn led to a level of intimacy we had never known together and, for me, an experience of devastation as I went through the inevitable process of weaning, for my original weaning had been so early and abrupt that I was filled with separation anxiety. This was a time of intimacy through intensity of experience and a time of real growth in our relationship. There were no holds barred and at times love and hate were indistinguishable.

In some ways our marriage is a conventional one. I am and have always been the main bread-winner and at times this has weighed heavily. The nuclear family kind of arrangement is not designed for intimacy and worldly matters can be both an intrusion and a defence against intimacy. The usual battlegrounds are money and sex, and we have had our fair share of those. But behind all these battles, I suspect, has been the need for real and authentic meeting and a healing of our individual deep woundedness.

Some woundedness comes from our upbringing, for example both having had parents who never really saw or heard us. Yet there is also an existential woundedness, the wound of aloneness. I had become very used to my aloneness, or more accurately, immured to my loneliness. This gave me the feeling of being an outsider, an outcast. Part of this world but not of it. I was certainly surviving but somehow I was sealed off, untouchable.

Frances, however, is not easily put off. In one of the early years, long before I had cancer, she did try to see me, but by that time I was unseeable, or so I thought. 'Don't look', I said, 'because there is nothing there,' and I believed it. Naturally, if one has never been seen, one cannot see oneself. If one has never been loved one cannot love oneself or another. Intimacy, in this context, seen is therefore seen as dangerous and threatening.

In Western society intimacy is built, not on the myth, but on the lie of romantic love. Mythology, however, tells us that it always ends in disaster. Eros and Psyche, Tristan and Isolde, Romeo and Juliet. Perhaps one of the truths that lies behind our continued fascination with these stories is an unconscious wisdom which recognizes that love is only really possible when one's heart has been broken; indeed, that a broken heart is a prerequisite for real intimacy.

In other ways, our marriage has been unconventional. For the first 10 years or so of having children, I was more at home than not and a very present father to our young. Later in that time they may well have felt excluded as we negotiated the turmoil of our relationship. Nevertheless, the one constant in our marriage has been the children: not that we have stayed together because of them, but that that is the one area where we have almost always been in agreement.

So what has really been the glue of our relationship? If I look at Frances herself, I am sure that her determination and tenacity, her perseverance and constant interest have been major factors. What has that to do with love, you may ask? That *is* love, I would reply. Her commitment came first – almost immediately, I believe. Mine came much later. In some ways I wish it had come earlier, for when one is not committed, there is always fear – the fear that the marriage will not work. Where there is mutual commitment, failure is not an option and fear diminishes. What follows is not just a determination to make the relationship work – that is, a commitment to the process itself and to the journey we are making together – but also an acceptance of 'what is'. Through that acceptance one can begin to see what is there in the other, rather than only what one perceives is lacking. It is then possible to take responsibility for anything which one perceives is missing, which will in turn enhance the relationship rather than threaten it. Perhaps that acceptance begins with self-acceptance and in recognizing, for example through good therapy, those childhood needs that were never met and the patterns that grow out of them. What I have always admired in Frances is her level of enquiry I am less enquiring by nature and she energizes that which I have. This can, however, be both stimulating and threatening.

As I write, I see more clearly the different levels of intimacy: the mental, the emotional and the sexual. Like most men, I have gone initially for intimacy through sex. Frances, I would say, has gone for intimacy through both mind and feelings. Part of the mystery of our relationship is that we survived the early years with little sexual fulfilment. The attraction to each other has certainly been there, but it was then of a different order. So we have not had the experience of many, who have a sexual blossoming which fades when the romance diminishes. Rather, through becoming intimate in other ways, mentally, emotionally and through life's experience, our sexual intimacy has grown. A fruit of our perseverance instead of an early blossoming. A later romancing.

Traditional marriage tends to be a no-growth system where the individual can be sacrificed to the relationship. Infidelity is often a sign that this is happening and that the marriage needs change. One of the hardest lessons I have learnt is to see that, for a relationship to survive and grow, the individuals within it have to grow too, so that what is infidelity in the marriage may be a big step of truth for the individual. This is the main reason for our high divorce rate, I would suggest: not the infidelity itself, but the difficulty we have in seeing the importance of growth for the individual *and* the system, and, of course, the difficulty of surviving the vengeance of a broken heart, the fading of illusion and, in many cases, the impossibility of coming to terms with betrayal. My bottom line is that self-betrayal is worse. Not that sacrifices are not necessary, they are, and that's the case in any relationship where one's partner's needs are important – but not at any price.

The moment we had children, their needs came first and the system of our marriage began to close. Indeed, the routine of home-making, child nurturing and bread-winning engendered a closed system. We had created this system in which I began to experience giving out more than I was receiving. Any system of relationship will crack eventually where there is too much self-sacrifice. An individual may break down, become ill, have an affair or leave. A betrayal of integrity occurs and this is necessary if there is to be any growth, whether it is happening within an individual, a couple or an institution. The closed system has to break, has to die in a way, for more to be included, just like a womb will eventually become suffocating to a baby if it is not born in time. My illness may have been the catalyst to break both my enclosed psychological and spiritual system and our constricting marriage. Other betrayals happened in the wake of that which shook our relationship to its foundations, but which opened up the closed system and allowed each of us and the marriage to grow. Nothing stays the same, yet one of the lies our Western civilization is built on is the view that there is such a thing as security and that security means keeping the status quo. In marriage or partnership change comes whether we like it or not. Betrayal seems to indicate a need for change or a shift in context. The context of a relationship changes the moment we have children and at various stages in between as they and we 'grow up' (I include the phrase 'grow down' – i.e. become more rooted in ourselves) and again when they leave home. We are now close to the latter stage and I would like to think that the emerging context in our relationship is happening more consciously and with our co-operation, rather than being forced on us by unconscious motivations.

As I see it, this new partnership will be more of a holding and supporting venture to our individual creativities, which is *being* together creatively. Whether we ever *do* anything creative together remains to be seen. Our children no longer need quite the same degree of creative input from us jointly as they used to.

If we are to spend another 25 years together, and as things stand there is the probability of that, and more, then the next stage of our partnership is going to be mostly without children.

Grandchildren perhaps, but that is a different story. If I look back at the past, I can see the full drama and saga of our lives together, the terrain and subterranean influences with which we have had to deal. There have been moments of great love and intimacy and those of painful separation. Whatever life throws at us now, I know we are better equipped to handle it, whether it be an external event or an internal one, even, or especially, when our unconscious agendas get triggered into action. Indeed, there is no one else with whom I would want to explore the second part of married life. It is a continuum, a journey through which I have come to know myself and my soul. A journey that might have happened with another but which has been with Frances. Through her, with her, because of her, and in spite or her, my life is measurably richer. I am learning about love in all its aspects. Like Beatrice, she has accompanied me into the underworld and back.

Earlier, I asked the question, 'What is the glue of our relationship?' It may seem odd that we are together after experiencing the thick and thin of our relationship, but that in itself could be a part of the ingredients which make the glue. There is something else, though, which is more difficult to speak about because it seems to transcend all of the experiences, transgressions, joys and memories. It is that intangible thread which is beyond any sense of emotional bonding. Certainly we are attached to each other and, as I see it, there is nothing wrong in that, provided one also knows what it is like to be separate or unattached. (To make non-attachment a preferred state, as in some Eastern traditions, only shows an attachment to non-attachment.) Indeed, knowing one can survive separation enables one to enjoy the attachment and open to the intimacy therein.

So what *is* the intangible quality of the glue? Is this a soul connection? The trouble with this realm is that its very intangibility defies explanation and is best expressed in art, poetry, music or metaphor, though most stories end when the drama of romance has climaxed, as if that is the end of it. Whereas for me, this is just the beginning. That there is a difference between soul and spirit I have no doubt. The soul of our marriage is that which has been and is being revealed to us all the time through the process of our relationship and in some of the ways I have suggested. It comes out of the experience of our relationship, the ups and downs, highs and lows. It brings meaning with it; it makes sense of our being together at all and it changes over time through that which is revealed about us individually and together.

The spirit of our relationship is something else. It is a constant. Something which never changes and yet something which seems to have been there (or here) all along, even in the darkest, bleakest moments. It is the energy which is obviously present when we enjoy one another, but still there, though dimmer, when we ask, 'Why are we still together?' It is therefore enduring, steadfast and, I suppose, unconditional. (I am not a fan of the words 'unconditional love' and to aspire to it seems to me as hierarchical and conditional as non-attachment is to attachment. Besides, most, if not all, human love is conditional, by which I mean that there is almost always some unconscious agenda involved.)

What I am attempting to describe is an ongoing and deepening sense of intimacy, not just of the moment, but something that matures over time. This brings an ease into the relationship which was not there before, which need not deteriorate into complacency or complaisance as long as one remains interested in the other. Like most men, apparent economic issues have grasped most of my attention and I have had to *learn* that the single most important aspect of my life is my relationship, coupled with the fact that as I grow and lead as creative a life as I can, that will enhance it. This maturity is not only about companionship but friendship. Companionship may not need truth, but friendship does and that can only happen between equals who sustain an interest in each other.

Frances has always had interest. She is a painter, an artist. I have learnt to be more enquiring, having learnt in childhood not to be. Together we have learnt to 'abandon [our] longing for the perfect', as Robert Bly puts it in one of his marvellous poems in *Loving a Woman in Two Worlds*. He adds:

> The inner nest not made by instinct
> will never be quite round,
> and each has to enter the nest
> made by the other imperfect bird.

I am certain, for the first time, that we can now enter each other's nests and love each other for the differences we find there, rather than wanting to change them to suit our own idea of perfection. What has built up over the years is trust. Not that I may not get hurt, but that I can survive that hurt. I even know I can survive if for any reason we may part. This is important because, even if it is death, one of us may be left alone. I am attached to Frances, but I am now in a position to handle any separation and the inevitable grief and no longer live in fear. Besides, what I would always have is her expression of love in the environment, not only in her paintings but in her unerring eye for colour and form in the home. We are both good home-makers but she has a gift for making any space an intimate one with utter simplicity and beauty.

Love and intimacy change over time. One of the delights of our growing older together is to see how we no longer take ourselves so seriously. A new intimacy is emerging, a playful one with more humour, which was sadly lacking before. As our relationship lightens, even though we have never seriously celebrated our anniversaries, our capacity to celebrate life increases. Not only on high days and holidays, but in every day.

Life is uncertain and never fully reveals its mysteries. My hope is that we continue together on this journey of discovery, in enquiry, in celebration, in strength and frailty.

Eileen & Michael Scott

EILEEN SCOTT

I have been married five or six times and divorced at least once, all to the same man. None of these 'happenings' have occurred legally, but all have reality in the psycho-spiritual domain.

I met Michael when I was at university. We both had many previous boy- or girl-friends (as they were called then). We were engaged for three years and after the parental opposition on both sides proved unrelenting (I was an only child, Michael the eldest, and cherished, son) we married and have, so far, been together for 36 years.

For me, my relationship to the other has finally been a journey into the Self. Not the small self of everyday doings, but that larger Self which governs my actions and at last is bringing peace and centredness beyond my expectations.

Our joint journey started in 1955, but its most important phase started 10 years ago, in 1981. Before then I had had a successful career in the world, if not a spectacular one. I started by taking a first degree in zoology and botany and then a M.Sc. in plant pathology. This led to lecturing in technical colleges, then to researching in industry with Michael when he came out of the Air Force. From that I progressed to running a marketing department and finally to strategic company planning.

At the age of 51, in 1981, I abandoned this career and negotiated early retirement. This was an ending that turned into a beginning. Recently I was looking at a poem that I had written in my middle years. It describes with great accuracy my state of mind at that time:

Slow creeping like a beggar without sight
The darkening of my life on a November night

We Two

It is sad to be alone
I place my feet carefully between the cracks
Of the wet grid paving stones
Sodium lamps yellowing the bronchitic street
No joy for me to linger
The dead brown leaves cling limpet to the curb
Obedient to mad winter
In shadowed doorways love fumbles promiscuous
And consummates the contest
The bright pedestrian globes stand high, strange wheat
My only barren harvest
I am one uncoupled conspicuous
Yesterday plans were fired
The ebb tide passes and I leave no tracks
For today bright dreams are tired.

This poem does not refer to the fact that in my early thirties I had two miscarriages which made me very ill, but rather to my psychic state. I had little desire for children. I was conforming to societal pressures, both at large and in the family, hence the physical near-disasters. Looking back at that time (of the two pregnancies), I would define my state as lacking in will, i.e. to be my own person. On the contrary, I was following the precepts of the 'Victorian will': I was doing my duty and following what I was told was my destiny as female rather than woman.

During my early thirties I used my will to make myself conform to what I perceived was expected of me. I felt guilty that I had little desire to procreate and was afraid of being categorized as failing as a woman. For myself, however, I saw self-realization in terms of a successful career and the development of any talents I might have.

I had no understanding, then, that societal norms are constantly changing, so that I had unnecessarily given myself fixed boundaries. I was operating from ignorance and thus gave myself few and limiting choices.

At the time I had two main emotions as a result of the pregnancies: one, an enormous relief that no children had resulted (I kept this to myself as an unacceptable opinion, or worse, that it might seem sour grapes); second, anger that I had followed a path so contrary to my basic nature. Now that I am old and no longer in danger from fecundity, I can enjoy children occasionally and can acknowledge that having a clan of many offspring might have its advantages: seeing the visible evidence of my genotype might well be satisfying.

It was many years before I could forgive myself for that whole episode. At the end of his book, *If You Meet the Buddha on the Road, Kill Him!*, Sheldon Kopp gives what he calls an 'Eschatological Laundry-list' of his eternal truths. For me, three of these truths resonate:

37 It is most important to run out of scapegoats.
41 You are free to do whatever you like. You need only face the consequences.
43 Learn to forgive yourself, again and again and again and again.

The last of Kopp's truths is very important to me. At last I have understood that the path of self-awareness, of awakening awareness, is endless: the mysterious journey is infinite. Also, I am slowly finding a different way of forgiving those apparently wasted years and those blind endings. I have realized that giving, or not giving, birth was just one of the many options forming the process of life. Discovering my Self seems, in retrospect, rather like peeling an onion with countless layers: one skin after another was exposed and discarded, with much tearful guilt, renunciation or anger at each shedding.

From midlife, 35, onward I suffered all the things that have at last been written about so extensively, such as constant fatigue and the feeling that nothing was worth doing and that nothing was relevant to me. I felt that I was living my life totally through the other, and 'where was I?' About this time I read *The Female Eunuch* by Germaine Greer and some of the numbness of disbelief and isolation began to disappear.

In 1981, soon after I left my job, I sat on the middle cushion of one of our sofas and made the following pronouncement (as Michael remembers it): 'I am going on a journey. I would like you to come with me. Even if you don't, I am going. It will change me, but I will still love you wherever this takes me.' The importance of this was twofold: I was fighting for my life and for a new marriage. I still do not know why it was so important to me when he said: 'I'll come with you.'

It is possible to describe the process of intimacy, even its nature, but totally impossible to explain the 'why'. We know about electricity, we use it in vast quantities. We can describe it as a flow of electrons from one electrode to another. But it is not possible to explain the mystery at the heart of things. Although I knew that I had to take a journey into the unknown, I cannot explain what alchemy within me, and between Michael and me, made it of such vital significance that we should continue together.

At the beginning of this early retirement I made some mistakes. I wrote a book on business practices which was not published. Then I learnt to use my painting and sculpting skills, becoming a professional artist. Although painting is still a way of exploration into myself, it has not been able to fulfil the needs of the journey. I was driven to read and read and read.

Someone once said: 'I read when I am empty, and I do not read when I am full.' My reading took me into strange territory but it was the right place. The books included all the 'awful' writings of Gurdjieff, his fractured English and digressions concealing as often as illuminating his truths, also the work of Ouspensky and the other apostles of this Sufi avatar. I read about reflexology, energy, chakras, auras, kundalini and meditation – all the literature that is to be discovered when the books of esoteric philosophy have been found wanting. None of it seemed difficult and I instinctively knew what most of it meant. Michael read the books and also understood, but was busy following his now highly successful business career just at the time that I had opted out. Now, as before, I felt isolated and, in the words of the wartime song, 'A lonely little petunia in a cabbage patch.'

In 1986, Michael's company was the target of a hostile takeover and, with the rest of the directors, he was made redundant. We were now together in a way that, until then, had seemed impossible. Synchronistically, I had found two men who were prepared to help me in my search for that inner Self. For the six months prior to the company takeover, Michael was in London trying to ward off the predator. To overcome what was then both physical and psychic loneliness, my search for the something else had become even more energetic.

A local organization specializing in self-development ran a course called 'Creative Listening' for those in the self-styled caring professions. I joined the course and found it such hard work that I often forgot Michael's business traumas and thought only of what I was doing. The course ran on into the early months of his retirement. One day he came in the car to collect me from one of the sessions. We were caught in a traffic jam and, as usual, he became angry. A great calmness descended on me: this had nothing to do with me. It was no longer necessary for me to try and smooth the path of the man I love. Here was another stepping-stone on the journey to separateness.

When the course finished I wanted the impetus of self-discovery to continue. I rang the man responsible for the course. We had not previously met. He is a psychotherapist. I said that I had read Gurdjieff *et al.* but could find no one to share my interest and I asked: 'Have you heard of these people?' The laugh at the other end was followed by an invitation to meet him. At the first meeting I said, 'I am not interested in delving into psychological problems. I want to work with energy.' I wished to explore those areas rarely discussed in our society except by those often categorized as the 'lunatic fringe'. His first question to me was: 'Are you grounded or are you up there?' – waving his hand about nine inches above his head. I said, 'Grounded.' 'Right,' he answered, 'then we'll start.'

After several months work, my guide and mentor said: 'I have a teacher who comes from Santa Fe and was trained at Esalen. He runs courses each year in this country; I think you should go.'

I always described this new work to Michael and I now told him that, if necessary, I would walk backwards all the way to Derbyshire for the week with this 'new master'. Fortunately, Michael decided that I should not go alone despite his misgivings about his own part in the process. In those days his loving protection contained a high degree of proprietorial control. When the new teacher met us he said to Michael, 'You give her a lot of space but then control her in that space.' He agreed, however, with Michael that this was reciprocal.

The work done in that precious week changed both of us in such a profound way that our future life would have been much different had we not been there together.

Much of the work during that week involved breaking the shackles of long-held beliefs, recognizing the connection between mind and body, learning that intellect is only one of our amazing abilities and that we have many other skills available. These skills can apparently be learnt by most people but for some mysterious reason are sought by only a few in every generation.

This experience proved to be an affirmation of my long journey. The redistribution of physical energies resulting from the process gave me the clarity to understand the meaning of the journey and where I was going.

Finding that internal centre of stillness, which may result from energy stabilization, meant the end of one way of looking at the world and for me resulted in acquiring a whole new set of concepts. As I went along 'The Road Less Travelled' with an intimate companion, I have no way of comparing its ease or difficulty with a solitary journey. What I do know, however, is that everything undertaken on this path of self-discovery is paradoxical: solitariness leads to unconditional love and this, in turn, leads to the knowledge that each jump into the unknown is an individual choice.

Within the intimacy of marriage there is the inhibition and retardation caused by social conspiracy, but on the other hand, there is loving support in times of crisis. It was inevitable that our transcendental change, which resulted from working with energy, led to analysis of the factors affecting our behaviour. Carlos Castaneda, in his series of books on 'the lessons of Don Juan' talks about the need for a 'petty tyrant' in the life of the 'impeccable warrior'. Michael and I have been each other's chief petty tyrants.

As I became more aware of my fantasies about my world, I was able to use the 'buttons' that Michael still presses in my psyche. When I feel that spurt of anger, that need to cry, that sudden descent into fatigue, I know that I am dealing with a complex of long-established behavioural patterns. Looking at these often leads me into that wonderful place of discovery of self and of the other.

As a result of the insights given by transactional analysis, neurolinguistic programming, dance, song, role playing, encounter, meditation, I can now trace the beginnings and endings of our five or six marriages.

First, there was the initial, amazing recognition and attraction: that blissful time when Michael was a 'knight in shining armour'. He could do no wrong, it was always the world that was out of step as far as I was concerned. I had no idea where our boundaries lay. The world and I glowed. I felt that I could achieve anything and that we could achieve anything together. For the first time, I felt truly cherished.

That first period ended one holiday. I did not want to join two other couples for a day's outing. Michael turned to me and said: 'You spoil everything and you never want to do anything.' I felt as though I had fallen down a mine-shaft. No longer were we one, he was now 'the other'.

What kept me in the marriage at that point? Physical passion, in part. In those days, sex education was minimal and there was certainly no discussion of sexual problems in society as a whole, so we had not discovered any. Beyond that was the determination to prove my family wrong – I had been invited to return home should I be unhappy. Never!

The second marriage was catalysed by my need to create a new relationship out of my wanting to love and be loved. It involved falling in love in a different way. Again, it was another form of identification with Michael. I thought he was brilliant, admired his mind and his many talents, both artistic and athletic. I was well trained. I gave up my chosen career to follow Michael into industry and we were employed by the same company to start up a research department. Even so, in the provinces in the 1950s this was not typical middle-class behaviour.

However, although nominally we were equal, in some way I had handed my 'marriage basket' to the other. His destiny became my destiny, his rise in society became my objective, his achievements made my striving on my own behalf unnecessary. It was not that Michael was unkind, or a tyrant; he was supportive of my ventures and made space for me. But I felt that I was on some predestined path that I barely understood and, worse, that there was no alternative.

Nowadays there are many books on this theme. Then,

women like me were brought up on a diet of anti-narcissism, put in our places by Freud and Jung. I was not able to be other than some form of male fabrication; any chance of appreciating myself as myself was pre-empted by the overriding concept of woman as an artefact of the male world. A series of female world leaders is beginning to forge a new role-model for women.

Onto the third marriage: a time of emptiness and despair epitomized in my November poem. That deeply-felt horror, 'This cannot be it, this cannot be the meaning of my life.' Michael was, by now, absorbed in his job and becoming more and more successful. My worldly ambitions were at an end. I had hit 'the glass ceiling'. In those days I could be told, and was, that I would be promoted no further because I was a woman.

During this time we bought a cottage, consisting of two rooms and a loft, to which we could escape from the pressures of his job. On Saturday evenings, over a bottle of wine, listening to the sea, we talked. Those Saturday evenings were highlights in an otherwise meaningless existence. I sometimes wondered whether I should leave that state, but where to go? What was there to find? I had no clue and no idea where to look.

The fourth marriage started the day Michael told me he intended to leave the company in which we had both worked, often very closely, for over 20 years. I could no longer escape the reality of 'the other' now that he had left our shared space as far as work was concerned. This gap in my life was very large. I had a choice as to how I could react. I might see things with complete pessimism (as with Caitlín Thomas's wonderful title for the book on her position following Dylan's death: *Leftover Life To Kill*) or, this time, actually search actively for some meaning. Even then, as in the first three marriages, I still tended to create a cage around myself, the bars of which were constructed from my fantasies which, in turn, were made from societal standards. I had despaired and been angry, had loved and been unhappy, but rarely on the terms that I knew existed somewhere.

And so we came to the fifth marriage, the time when Michael was retired too. This is the time when we have found out how to explore our togetherness and our separateness. This is the time of growing, excitement and fulfilment.

An unexpected bonus was finding others bent on the same quest. It was, and is, remarkable how much work is going on in the area of self-fulfilment. We found that a number of organizations and individuals were offering the opportunity to work together, using a wide range of new and old methods for discovering and expressing the true self.

Someone we know said to us: 'How do you two ever stop processing?' The answer is that we don't, we do not want to – so much to learn, so many fantasies to dismantle. As our wise old man from Santa Fe said, 'This is *my* world – which, of course, does not stop it being *your* world.' My world is everything I create, everything I am, dream, destroy or save.

Suddenly, six months ago, we found that we could not even ask for the marmalade without provoking dislike: every word was misunderstood, even the 'ands' and 'buts' were libellous. Was this where all our work had led; to separation and failure? Then Michael said: 'It's the marriage, the marriage is the cuckoo in the nest. Maybe we have to jettison this third element in our lives and become two people who just want to be together.' It was an invitation to a feeling from age-old fantasies. I entered into that invitation.

It was not necessary to have a dramatic legal separation. There was nothing to be gained by it. We both wanted to go on living together. Now, although we have agreed we have no marriage, we seem to have the strongest of the marriages. My perception is that we are free from decisions made in the name of the abstract called 'marriage' and of expectations that do not necessarily coincide with our truths.

How have we come through all this? I do not know. I can only tell you the process. We are part of a dream, where we both seem to have been living the archetypes of the age, living the growing pains of the century, where men and women struggle to a new consciousness. How can I tell you about the ecstasy of love, of loving one person above all other? How can I lead you to the journey, that shows you that you have to love yourself above all others before you can truly love? All I can say is that on this journey into me I have found the Other and the Sacred.

MICHAEL SCOTT

Relationship is a game, sometimes deadly, in which we play around with reality. As there is no such thing as Reality, only my reality, your reality, his reality, the game is infinitely confusing to the players. To make it even more interesting, it is doubtful, though not certain, whether the game actually exists at all. There is a view, which I find hard to fault, that when we have a relationship with someone we are really only having a relationship with our own self. Everything I read into the other is only a reading into myself. Then the other shouts at me, throws a plate on the floor, embraces me, whatever, and there does seem to be something out there after all.

All through my life, however, I have experienced a sense of unreality in relationship. 'Whose reality am I in?' is the question that repeatedly asks itself. My first very important one-to-one was with a woman called Hilda. I think I dwelt within her reality, rather than mine, for about 15 years. During that time she was the core of my existence and even now, decades later, I have a problem in sorting out who I belonged to, what I was, during my love affair with Hilda.

Such a relationship, where the game is played according to the rules of the dominant player, leaves the weaker partner in a daze. Was she real? Did she really do that? Why am I unable to remember much about her, considering how much I loved her? It's like a lost weekend lasting 15 years. Also, what kind of shape is one in for subsequent relationships? How did that one, if it really existed, actually end?

All these questions are unanswered, 45 years after that love-affair ended and 22 years after Hilda's death. In that long interval we had a non-relationship. I do not know whether, or how much, we continued to need one another for those 23 years during which we met, kissed, hugged, talked, recriminated, and drifted apart. One thing is sure, somehow there is still a gap in my life marked 'mother'.

From 15 to 20 years of age, while Hilda was trying to hold me and I was running towards imagined freedom, I pursued many young females. What could I offer them, in terms of relationship? Virtually nothing, as I recall it. But, presumably, they failed to offer me much, also, in that area. Nubility, teasing, frustration, jealousy, lust, idealization, anger, boredom, not much else, was what these 'relationships' gave me. By the time I was 24 I was already a cynical old man.

Desire was all right, as far as it went, which was not very far, but where was this love all those songs and poems and novels were bleating about? More and more unreality. Was this IT?

Then came Eileen. She and I looked sceptically at one another and then she put on a long white dress and a man wearing a short white dress said we were man and wife. Hilda did not like this at all. She never came to terms with this new relationship of mine. Her not coming to terms with it seemed unfair to me, in my reality. In hers, who knows? I would have liked to have been cosseted and worshipped by Hilda and Eileen, but it was not that difficult to accept that a choice had been made at a level beyond my comprehension.

All this about my mother has relevance in that my first passionate relationship with a woman finished up in such a dreary state. I was pre-programmed for relationship problems. It was obviously 'difficult' to make a woman happy, and my pride was such that I was absolutely determined that Eileen should be happy with me. I worked hard at it. I loved her and loved her. I still do, right down to my roots and right up to my transpersonal self. In the love department, there is no shortage of love.

But, understanding and awareness? Well, that is another story. Which story should I tell? The one about 36 years of monogamous, single-minded devotion to one woman, sickness and health, poor and not so poor, till death us do part? Or the one about two confused people, trying to understand each other, trying to make things good for each other, trying one another's patience to breaking point, giving up and then trying some more, playing in this hopelessly complicated game called 'Relationship'?

The easy part is: it is the same story. It only becomes two stories, or three, or 30, if you play the many reality-ploys at your disposal.

At the great conjunctions of our long game, when we have reached the depths or the heights of emotion (and both have happened very often), the really extraordinary thing is how well we have treated one another. I am amazed by the sweet wells of kindness that were always there, between us, even and especially when we seemed to be at the furthermost pitch of loathing for one another. What always seems to happen, in our ecstasy, in our pain, or in our everyday muddling along, is a sense of compulsion towards more loving.

How it is, then, that having failed to maintain a 'satisfactory relationship' as a son, after being a philanderer with a dozen or so girls and jilting the one of them whom I had loved the most – thereby ending five years of precarious passion – I should have subsequently played the relationship game with such earnestness and such constancy for nearly four decades? What has Eileen got that no one else ever had? What have I found in myself for her which was conspicuously absent before I married her?

I would have to admit that being *married* is part of the answer. There is something atavistic operating in that 'holy' contract.

But it is not a large part of the answer, for me. I am anti-religious and pro-spiritual, so the sacred nature of marriage is not so much ordained as something requiring persistent effort and attention. If marriage is to be a sacred connection then it must receive its grace from the openness and willingness of the two participants; their openness to the individuality of each other and their willingness to accept dual autonomy rather than mutual control and ownership.

The spirituality of *this* marriage was, however, a long time growing. It was many years before we were able to perceive, let alone form, that full sacred connection. There must have been a strong bond which held me to her, and her to me, which was more than the marriage vows, if less than full spiritual partnership.

If I say she replaced Hilda, it may be thought that I had a mother-complex: that I needed to be controlled, cossetted and reassured by a surrogate mother. I would not deny some degree of that. I rather like the idea. It does not stand up to scrutiny, however, because Eileen is the least maternal woman I have ever known. This tempts the opposite interpretation: that the bond was strong because she was so far from being a second mother. Who knows?

The sense in which she may have replaced Hilda is more likely that I was able to move into a totality of loving with her which most resembled that first wonderful bond when I was a boy. The atavism is thus more like the sense of: 'This is the one, the only one, and for ever', as a mantra deep in my being.

Because we have no children we have no bonds of that kind. But this has been an advantage. Children can be a wonderful excuse for staying with someone you have come to detest. The relationship between the adults has been suborned by their relationship with the children. Or they split up and continue to suffer the pangs of incomplete parenthood. For us, we have only ever had the stark reality of each other, without the confusion and compulsion of 'possessing' small humans who would eventually leave us to become themselves.

Not that I am pleased not to be a father. But for a long time, and perhaps still, I would consider myself unsuitable for the role. I look at what happens in families, the terrible pain arising from the real or supposed awfulness of the father, and part of me is grateful for not being someone's source of self-damage. Yet, another part says: 'Oh, wouldn't it be good to be close to someone who could be with Eileen and me in the extraordinary and special way that some families have with one another!'

Sometimes I will see a little child and feel the power in it to draw from me the deepest and most reverent commitment, but it 'belongs' to someone else: I wish it countless blessings.

The truth is that, until now, my ability to love a child might have been damaging to the child and to myself. I would have been possessive, controlling, anxious, demanding, generous and selfish. The child would have been over-fathered, too loved, too important. It has had a lucky escape – and so have I.

The lack of children does not seem to have been relevant in my long affair with Eileen. It is as if we have a path to walk together which has needed each of us to search and search for the essence of our two selves so that there could be, eventually, a dedication to something beyond parenthood and the other ordinary things of this world. That search is hard and long and I am certain that a son or a daughter would not have made much difference to it, except to have added to the excuses for not persisting in the struggle for wholeness.

Sexuality is certainly a major element. But it needs to be seen in a rather special light. In my experience there are at least two separate modes in operation. There is the attractiveness of women generally, and then there is the attractiveness of The One. They are two quite different manifestations of Eros. A long-lasting relationship is one in which the major erotic key is being played. So, it happens that Eileen is the woman for whom I feel that particular form of sexual charisma, as if she were a Circe to my Odysseus. Even this metaphor is significant. We are both conscious of the fact that our lives have taken on the nature of journeys in these last years. In my odyssey into my self, Eileen has become an increasingly important magical reference point.

I am not sure how two 60-year-olds are supposed to represent themselves in the sexual field of combat. The erotic part of the relationship game generally seems to me to be the joker in the pack. The more a relationship is centred upon its physical sexuality, the more it wanders from its consecration. I speak as one whose sexual impulse has been almost unbearably powerful. Our early years together were very physical and I remember those ecstatic contacts with the greatest joy. Yet, it is now that our sexuality is reaching its fullest expression.

The touching of hands, the stroking of a cheek, a gentle kiss; how could the 25-year-old Michael have known the treat in store for him in his oldish age? The temple of Eros has many chambers. When I see the desperate struggle of ageing people to make their bodies look and behave as if they were 30 years younger, I wonder whether they will ever discover those secret inner places of the sexual spirit.

In some ways, Eileen and I are at our best when we are playing the relationship game to its most dangerous and dirty limits. There is a wayward quality in both of us which pushes us to take risks. Often, the game becomes poker. We bluff a lot. How far can I push her, how far will she take me? We laugh at one another a lot, too. Even the laughter is a try-on, sometimes. I am saying, I suppose, that part of the magical attraction that has stood the test of so many years is the fact that we are prepared to be opponents when the game demands it.

We also bring out the best in one another. When we co-operate on something – interior decoration, a painting, a poem, a meal, a group exercise – the result is always better than we could achieve separately.

Someone once dubbed us 'The Heavenly Twins'. I can see how we might appear: two naughty, collusive children who will create mayhem for themselves and everyone else and find the result endlessly interesting. Yes, there is that aspect, to be sure.

But this still does not get to the essence of our togetherness. I come closer to it if I look at the enormous demands we have always made of one another. At a very early stage in our 'game' I realized that Eileen had invested her whole universe in me, and that I had put a similarly ludicrous burden upon her. Our 40-year voyage together has been very largely about taking back those burdens from one another.

My personal path of progression through the minefield of male achievement has been a constant inspiration and irritation in our relationship. Every success has been a problem. I could see how Eileen was being nullified by my easy, though not so easy, rise through the patriarchal ranks. Often I was apparently showered with honours and other nice things, which she would have given several precious teeth to have for herself. She worked hard to achieve commensurate rewards but, of course, it is different for a woman, men only fight fair against men – except that they actually don't.

Now even all this playful horror did not really dent us. We hated it, of course. But there were vast areas of inner commitment which easily absorbed these miseries. The more we suffered the better we became.

Each of us could write a litany of the anguish suffered as a result of The Relationship. Indeed, several poems and midnight essays exist to prove the amount we have wept and raged about one another.

If we were let loose in a divorce court – provided it was still a game – we could give everyone a run for their money. But why should we entertain others when we give each other so much enjoyment?

How was it possible that all this fighting was serving any useful purpose? What makes me say that we have benefited from the suffering? The answer is that it was, at a lowish level admittedly, a working-through of the basic dedication. We were such huge presences for one another, great archetypal manifestations, that we were compelled to give each other all we had – good and bad.

I regret, now, the awful lack of comprehension in our jousting. Our education, from five to 25 years of age for each of us, had equipped us to be cleverly stupid, to value intellectual brilliance and achievements, to win in the world. So our battling stance extended to each other on occasions when we would have been wiser to surrender. Also, our love so often expressed itself as a need, a demand, a claim or a complaint.

Nevertheless, all this was rather like two fox-cubs, albeit getting on a bit, mock-fighting in preparation for their short, hard, adult life. At 30, or 40, we were still children, practising grown-up games. Sooner or later, the chance to be adult would present itself. The long wrestling-match had made us strong, in some ways, but also vulnerable, and damaged. The marriage was, in its way, successful. We were ready to move on: out into the (extraordinary) world.

There was, then, that one matter which had both held us together all this time and yet threatened to drive us, ultimately, apart. This was the true core of the relationship, the serious part of the game. This was the question of the Real Self.

As our chronology edges towards the final precipice, the question of who I am and what am I going to do about me becomes urgent. I saw that Eileen had got to that

Overwhelming question; Oh! do not ask what is it

when I was still hoping I might not have to ask it. It is now a few years since I really yelled the question to the stars. At last, the long odyssey of the two voyagers makes sense. As poor Parzival discovered, almost too late, it is all a matter of asking the right question (and not so much finding the right answer, which in the best of games does not actually exist).

Parzival, the 'Great Fool', had entered the world of combat and chivalry, entranced by its glory. Eventually, faced with the wounded Fisher King, he remembered his manners and politely ignored the suffering of his host. This was the turning-point of his quest. He had failed to ask the King what 'ailed' him.

After this, he trailed on for years, in a wilderness of despair, not knowing how to solve this problem of being: how to find his spontaneous, truthful voice at the critical moment. At last, of course, he did: in his final great battle he had all but overcome an equally powerful knight, only to find that it was his exotic brother, half black, half white. He was, at the end, fighting himself. It was time to stop, and claim his destiny.

Eileen was a female Parzival who had reached her point of destiny earlier than me. Her gallant, chivalrous progression through domestic and worldly battles had reached its climax. She was now on a different route. I went on, for a while, clanking around in my uncomfortable armour, falling off my horse, getting bruised and battered. The 'wins' were becoming less and less worthwhile: I needed to join her on this new path, but it was still to be a few years before I was able to face my self and say to it 'Why am I fighting you?'

But I did begin to stop doing it. Between Eileen and myself, the contests went on for a while, but they were changing and diminishing. Such contests as occurred were now definitive, reaching for full maturity. We each realized this was our last chance to move into a relationship which would empower each of us, give space and autonomy, allow love to grow to its full potential.

What, then, had we been trying to do all these years? I could now see Eileen reaching for a self-affirmation which was much greater than herself. It was not just a matter of understanding the bodymind, the esoteric energy patterns of the human form, and the half-forgotten roots of healing experience, though these were implicitly involved. Somewhere in our psyches there was an even older and deeper drive. It is the power of the Sacred Other.

As I have said, I am not religious. By that I mean I cannot find anything that truly touches me in any of the world's big or small cults and dogmas. I dislike the very idea of belief. It limits the human imagination and pre-empts any future manifestation of the ineffable mystery of the universe.

But, the Sacred Other is another matter. It seems that I have always been aware of an essence of something beyond the play of our various human games. In my early days, a proper humanism made me restrict the idea to the realm of living people and the wisdom and artefacts of our ancestors. I would have said that everything I cared for was human, though I preferred plants and animals as general acquaintances. This belief made me very miserable.

In Eileen I found a person I could almost deify, which was a very bad mistake. Yet the impulse had some sense in it. She was an embodiment of the Sacred Other, as we all must be if this idea means anything. To worship the Sacred Other from afar is a safe but pointless project, because you never get really tested. I recognize the agonies of the religious ecstatics, and suspect they are in similar territory because of the sharpness with which they perceive the presence of their god. However, I started my ecstatic career with a real, flesh and blood, holy female.

If Abelard had kept his genitals and stayed with Heloise he might have become a fully pious man. I am suspicious of holy men who abjure the company and intimacy of a loving woman. For me, after the early experience of my mother as the Sacred Other, it was essential that I should be able to be with someone else who tested me to destruction and that I should survive. For someone to have that role for me they must be intrinsically formidable but also able to receive and handle my projections upon them. This asks a lot and takes time, one reason why a long relationship is needed.

Projection, as with Parzival in his relationships with others, is the way we see in others our own feelings, needs, aspirations. He saw everyone, until he recognized his mistake, as vehicles for his own knightly behaviour. In my relation with Eileen, she embodied my aspirations, dreams, fears, and assumptions about the ideal female. Every time the real Eileen tried to break through, I would stubbornly persuade her to go back into the beautiful caricature I had created for her. No excuses for this – it is only romantic love, after all; and she was making the equivalent fantasy for me to fit into.

The awful thing is that we knew, in our heads, all about this nonsense. We laughed at it in others, in films, books, plays. Yet, until we could get to the place of surrendering our need for everything to reflect our desires or aversions, we could not *feel*, and thus *act* against this projection.

The term 'projectionist' for the person who manages the equipment in a cinema is an apt label: it is just like that, making a moving picture 'out there', and making it 'The Reality'. To change this takes time, even if you have the will to change it. The reason for changing it is so that the sacredness inherent in a relationship is freed from the crushing weight of fantasy. And one's own sacredness also takes time, and good fortune, to reveal itself.

In the past, I had experienced many 'peak experiences', as they are called, in which there appeared to be an otherworldly presence about me. But unless these are systematized into an exoteric cult they tend to get 'parked' in one's memory. Then, one day, they have to be brought out of the cupboard and honoured for their collective significance.

The cumulative effect of recent years is that the dossier of inexplicable experiences has to be merged with the moves that are now being revealed in the relationship game. Overall, the subjective evidence is overwhelming: the Sacred Other is real. Like the Self with a capital 'S', there really is something there, a shape in the undergrowth like Castaneda's moth which was a terrifying ally.

Castaneda, the narrator in a series of 'novels' describing his prolonged apprenticeship to the teacher-sorcerer, Don Juan, was repeatedly taken to 'the brink of himself' where total self-awareness was possible. On this brink, there is a wide variety of influences – energy, spirituality, nature, relationships, fear, desire – which may push a person to 'jump into the void' and there experience an entirely new reality. The 'ally' was one of these influences, neither quite a projection nor entirely an external entity, which was inviting/pushing Castaneda toward self-revelation and greater power.

In my life, as with Castaneda, I have been confronted often by a presence of some kind which has made a demand of me quite beyond my everyday comprehension. Castaneda was very frightened of the dark, huge shape in the bushes because he was, even after many years of Juan's teaching, still an ego-bound fool. In my case, these presences have become less scary as my foolishness has diminished; and what at first might seem horrible monsters are benevolent friends when allowed to enter the living-room of the self.

The 'foolishness' of Castaneda, or myself, or everyone else, is the need, the determination, to understand everything and to fit it into one's tidy box of assumptions and beliefs. As with giant moths in the bushes, so with a beloved partner. That great presence in, and around, Eileen is not to be easily understood, docketed, pinned in place in my mind. The wonderful *otherness*, at all the levels, affirms me so long as I am able to affirm it. Once you really accept that nothing is real, everything is real.

As far as I know, Parzival was not in a position to be helped by great art; though, ironically, the genius author Wolfram von Eschenbach who wrote the Parzival epic was himself a knight, living in the late twelfth century – so he, at least, knew how art (as poetry) could open windows which might otherwise remain closed.

Music has opened windows for me for many years. At first, I was emotionally moved by music, 'entranced', as in my early relationship with Eileen. Then, in time, music began to make deeper demands – as did she. In a miraculous way, these things are now coming together: the Sacred Other is present in music, poetry, painting as It also is in the intimate relationship with a person.

To go, for example, into the utter unreality of Mozart's *Figaro* is to experience this Sacred Other. It is possible, I suppose, to experience this opera as a story, set to music, of an aristocrat's attempt to exercise his 'noble right' to ravish the fiancée of his servant. At one level it is a political drama. At another, it is a *risqué* comedy of sexual manners. But, for me, it has become quite something else: the Sacred Presence that may enter into the relationship between human beings.

Like the long game with Eileen, I never know where It will happen. Even in my own recordings, the Presence comes in different places at different hearings. I may expect to be moved to ecstasy by the Countess's aria only to find it is in the Count's ravings that the magic happens. I watched a recent performance in which my moment of transfixing was the nonsense around dressing Cherubino in woman's clothes. He, played by a she, is turned into a she, while she/he ogles and preens to the two women dressing her/him.

My growing sense of the Sacred Other feeds on Mozart, Strauss, even Mahler; music has the inherent power of bringing me into that state or presence of sacred relationship. I watch a bird feeding its young, a child talking to her father, two lovers on the beach, Eileen smiling at a friend: the mystery is everywhere.

If I look for the Sacred Other, it stays hidden. If I sit and wait for its appearance, it plays in the sunlight and the shade, teasing me. It is always around, in everything, real and unreal. Then

I will be standing before a human other, and we will look at one another, and the sacredness will suddenly be there between us.

It is inclusive and not exclusive. The more I experience the Sacred Other in my games with Eileen, the more it appears in my games with other beings. The Count and Figaro are set up against one another by every device of male egotism and eroticism. Yet, on that stage, sometimes, they will look at one another as human essences and the Sacredness of their being will shine around them for a moment.

I watch people in workshops, playing through their fantasies, and marvel at the way the Sacredness will suddenly be there. It is as if the human spirit is itself a grail in which the Sacred Other can be become manifest. The magical quality in my life is the experiencing of that manifestation.

As in Castaneda, some 'stalking', some 'dreaming', some 'seeing' is required. In the wonderful relationship game I have played together with Eileen for so many years, the Sacred Other has been the reality within the unreality and the unreality within the reality. Now, more than ever, the Game is the thing and I hope to play it until the very end. At that very end, it will be the Sacred Other that I hope to see, for the thousandth time, to make it a celebration, not an ending.

Marion Woodman

EMBRACING THE DARK

MW I am glad to see that some of the stories in this book mention the difficulties of people trying to live out a new paradigm in relationship. It's all well and good to talk about individuality and people maturing through their relationship, but the old models are deep in our bones and to try to move into a new way of relating is very threatening.

RH Threatening to . . .?

MW It's threatening because the old parental complexes are still clinging on. A man who has not worked very hard on his mother complex, for example, is still going to look for the security and nourishment of the mother and is still driven to please the mother, unconsciously. Unconscious means unconscious. People forget that. A man may say, 'I am no longer tied to the mother; I do not try to please her.' But on the unconscious level that need to please can be overwhelming. If he doesn't please her, he may feel he is going to be destroyed. The mother complex takes on the form of the wife, or the corporation or university on which he is dependent for a living.

It is the same for a woman with a father complex. She may feel that she has to say YES to a man in the smallest details. Then when she finds herself standing up and saying NO, it makes her sick in her stomach, it makes her almost faint. I'm talking now about the unconscious level, where there's something touching into the archetypal security at the basis of the personality. It feels like the ultimate rejection and the ultimate abandonment; she is putting herself in the position where the person who loves her most may put her out. At the archetypal level, of course, that ties in with God. She fears God will reject her. Or in the man's case, the Goddess will reject him.

CG So what would the woman's creative response be to that situation?

MW She must work extremely hard to overcome that. She must always try to stand up for her own values. She cannot simply say, 'I'm not going to vomit.' It doesn't work. I have known women who were divorced 12 years ago who are still dreaming about their husband, their 'ex', and they say, 'Why do I still dream about him? He's gone from my life, I couldn't care less about him.' But obviously he's there, and if something obliges the parents to meet again – some arrangement or discussion over the children, for example – she may feel so ill she thinks she has food poisoning.

Then all the old stuff about lying and pretence comes up. Certainly if there is a psychotic corner anywhere it comes up. The psychotic corner evokes the terror that is totally irrational, totally immature. It is the corner which often binds two people into a relationship that makes them utterly dependent on each other. People will stay in a relationship that is quite destructive because they cannot deal with the tiny infant, the one that is totally dependent on mother or father. So, when the 'ex' reappears, that's the terrified part that comes up. You have to work at a deep level to heal that.

To answer your question, it takes great courage. Often you just have to whisper 'no', and be aware of all the terror that is in your body; and often you fail. At that point you have to say, 'OK, I failed in that encounter. In the next encounter I may win.' And, gradually, you foresee where the problems happen. I think that through journaling you can keep saying to yourself, 'This is where I always catch the projection. This is where the male constellates the infant in me, and this is where I project onto him.' Bring it to consciousness. The next time it happens you may be able to say what you want to say, instead of falling into the unconscious and going along with what you've always done. This is the hardest task in a new kind of relationship.

I don't think you ever get totally free. I think that it's foolish to think that you'll completely overcome it. It circles around even in our boss; we often meet the judgemental mother or the judgemental father in a job. In so many different ways we run into it until we're clear, if we ever are. It's amazing how, as we get older and more vulnerable, these things start to recircle and the little child in the relationship comes up. We have to be very discriminating as middle age and old age come on because, as our bodies become weaker, we do need to have that child taken care of. If one partner is sick, that child has to be nurtured. Sometimes we want to roar out, 'I'm not your mother . . . I'm not your father.' It's hard, and we have to be discriminating in every situation. Opening to love allows the child to mature.

I also think that, when the old patterns start to take over, you have to get away from each other, even momentarily, to recover your own ground. Otherwise, your ego will gradually fall deeper and deeper into unconsciousness, the old patterns will continue to exert themselves and, once that happens, you are lost. When that is happening, you separate for an hour or however long you need to find your own ground, then come back in dialogue with each other and perhaps bring in the anger.

I don't believe in getting into anger that goes into rage. Rage has to do with an archetypal dimension and most of us have centuries of rage in our bones. Once you get to a certain point in anger, something else starts to take over and you are no longer saying what's coming out of your mouth. Then it's murder with words. I've had many women say to me, 'I don't know what got into me. He didn't deserve at all what I gave him. Poor creature just stood there and took it.'

That tears a relationship to pieces. It's pointless. Rage belongs in a therapeutic situation. If you are paying professionally to work with your depths, let rage out in the session, or work with it with somebody who knows how to deal with it. It has no place in a relationship. Anger, however, does, because you are present in your anger. If you are a conscious person you understand when you are angry and you are mature enough to dialogue. But if you are in rage, then you are possessed and not present.

Now, of course, all this depends on the individual couple. The more conscious you are, the less danger there is of falling into the unconscious patterns, but you have to be willing to recognize that some of those old patterns are going to recur. You must forgive yourself and forgive your partner because you can't become conscious overnight. A new dawn doesn't necessarily bring a new light in the psyche. One of the saddest examples would be the partners who have lived together for five years not wanting to get married because they don't like the old stereotypes and then, for one reason or another, they do marry and the sexuality goes wrong almost immediately. Stereotypically, they suddenly become mother and father in the marriage bed. Then the instincts pick up on that and act accordingly, causing a sexual difficulty at once. That has to be brought into consciousness or it will get worse, and they will see themselves re-enacting the marriages of their parents – the very thing they tried so hard to avoid.

Marriage and Monogamy

MW There are legal marriages and sacramental marriages. If a couple accepts the divine sacrament of marriage, then each believes that in the sacrament a miracle takes place and the two become one flesh. To be unfaithful to that creates a fearsome tearing apart. Now I am sure there are some couples who have that sense of one flesh without the sacrament. There are others who are miraculously surprised by it. 'We thought we were married before, but this is something totally different.'

Somehow, the two energies are interacting in a different way because there has been a sacrament. I can think of examples where this has happened to friends. They had what they believed was a sacramental relationship without marriage. Then they began to fight and there was a constant wrangling. They were edgy all the time. And when they saw that they were in a sacred relationship that had not been recognized as sacred, they got married and the fighting stopped.

RH Who was it not recognized by, though? Whose recognition did they need?

MW They needed their own recognition beyond the personal relationship.

CG And that was established through the medium of the public witness?

MW No, I think they could have gone to church without any public witness at all, but deep somewhere in them the ritual itself was part of their life, and when it came to this most sacred of relationships they needed a ritual to say this is recognized in the eyes of God. And then they trusted at a new level of trust – a level beyond themselves. The relationship is no longer two people in love, but two people loving each other through God. The third is at the centre of the relationship. As in dancing, some people dance with each other; other people become the music and the dance is free and spontaneous, every minute new. It is not the recognition of the fathers and mothers or the public or the friends. It's a heart knowing.

Now I also appreciate the value of the unmarried, literally the 'outlaw', status of the unmarried couple. I think that a lot of married couples whose children have left move into this place. They have to go through a hard transition to find the new relationship that is essentially outside the traditions belonging to marriage in order to keep their relationship alive and creative. They really have to let each other go and, in letting go, they find a new love for each other. In fact, if you stay within a marriage, there is going to be a new marriage forming all the way along, at different age levels. One of the couples in this book points this out. You are a very different person at 40 than you were at 25, and a whole new set of premises has to come in if the marriage is to survive and grow.

RH One of the intentions of this book has been to listen for new models, new intuitions of relationship that are beginning to emerge in the culture. Do you have any comment on that?

MW I'll tell you one model that I am seeing often. Some couples are together three or four days a week and spend the rest of the week apart. They have the joy of being together and the equal joy of being alone, finding themselves through their inner discovery, and working in the creativity of their job. Then they take all of that back into the relationship.

RH That brings up the whole conflict and sometime compatibility of two myths. That is, the romantic myth of our togetherness and the myth of me, my growth, my individuality. And perhaps that's one of the major changes of the last 20 years, that the individual sense of destiny and purpose, especially among women, has been coming to the surface, challenging the automatic assumption of the myth of 'us'. So the model you have just mentioned sounds like a way of embracing these two myths.

MW Yes. I think that many people can't hold consciousness seven days a week, and therefore they fall back into the complexes. By being away from each other for three or four days, they are able to re-establish, to reaffirm who they are, clear of a complex. When they go back to the partner they can work within that new recognition of themselves. Now, I think that some people are not doing that at all. They are allowing themselves the self-indulgence of falling into the unconscious for the three days they are home. There they fall back into the old romantic thing. She becomes the perfect little doll, and he becomes the perfect dad. Or she is the perfect mother and he is the beloved son. They live out the romanticism of *puer* and *puella*, eternal idealization. They live out the romanticism together and then they go off and try to be their individual selves. Now, that is a Jekyll and Hyde split. That will reinforce any addictive behaviour. They realize that, when they are going back on the train to work, they can feel their body changing; they may have a different set of clothes; they may have a totally different metabolism. And then, when they know it's time to go home, again the change of clothes, the metabolism shifts, and they go back into their other personality. It is schizophrenic. Sometimes, of course, there can be another person involved.

RH You must be seeing some conscious or positive attempts at marrying these two myths as well.

MW Sure, I think that some people are working very hard while they are alone; working on their journal or doing whatever they need to do with their bodywork to try to find their own reality. And when they go back to the partner they try to live that reality and usually there is a terrific fight because one or other is going to say, 'You're not the person I married.' Well, that's true. You see, so long as your partner is absent you can project anything onto them. But once they're standing there right in front of you, speaking things that you don't believe they're capable of saying, you have to deal with it. And you can either blind yourself to the creature standing in front of you and talking, or you can say, 'I have no idea who you are, but I am willing to try to find out. I don't know whether I'm going to love you or not when I know who you are. And I'm not sure either if you're going to love me when you know who I am.' But you really do have to learn all over again to love. This time, another; not your image of another. Most people are in love with their own projected image. What they call love is a narcissistic falling in love with their own projected, contrasexual self. They may even hear their own echo. Sometimes, if they don't see their own image and hear their own echo in the other person, they go off and find another.

RH What is your response to the question of monogamy?

MW I think that if you are true to the core of the other person, monogamy is in that truth. It's very difficult . . . I am not even sure I believe that as I say it, because I know that so many people I am working with have met someone – a third person – who brings out a totally different aspect of their personality. Something that was repressed in them, something that they didn't know at all, is brought to life by that other person. The projection happens and they say, 'It would be death for me not to experience this.' I understand that; on the one hand, they might be sending themselves to sleep for the rest of their lives, and on the other, this might be where destiny is wanting to enter, to open life. For them to experience the totality of themselves, they may have to experience that other person. Often, it is the pain of the conflict that brings them to a whole new understanding of who they are. The suffering involved opens them up to their own humility, to forgiving themselves and other people. I think it is possible for a man or a woman to be able to say with honesty, 'I love my marriage partner and I love this other person, and loving this other is not changing my relationship to my partner, except I think I love them more than I ever did.' The other relationship can open up a whole new part of themselves that they can bring back into the marriage – as one of the couples in this book reveals. It can be a real possibility for growth; at the same time, it is bound to create suffering.

I would also say that there is a morality in the unconscious that is just as strong as the laws of consciousness; but it is different. It has to do with being true to the soul. I think it has to do with how one is related to the embodied soul. Having an affair is one thing for people who consider their body a sacred temple in which their soul lives, quite another thing for people unrelated to their soul in their body. An extreme form would be the prostitute. Her allegiance is not to the men she is having sex with; her allegiance and her love are often for the man she is working for. That is an extreme example, but, like the prostitute, many people do not value the soul connection in the body. They may have an intense disembodied soul connection with someone, and whatever affairs go on cannot touch that, and therefore present no threat, because soul and body are split apart. The dream process attempts to make the person whole, and the morality of the unconscious leads in that direction, trying to bring love and lust together.

CG Can we turn to the question of honesty in relationships?

MW Things are changing, but most people are still afraid, women in particular, to say what they really feel. Most women are afraid to express their real value. They know what patriarchal thinking is, and they know how their husband thinks; in their effort to keep the marriage running smoothly, they do everything to please rather than speak up and say what they think. Or they remain silent, which is the same thing. Then, way on down the line, they blame their husband for not seeing who they are. He never had a chance to see who his wife is because she has not spoken her reality. This is also true for the man who is trying to please the mother in the wife–mother. The upshot is they become two strangers and neither one, in their efforts to please the other, is doing what they want to do.

George Bernard Shaw talked about a marriage in which one partner wanted to go west and the other east. They end up going north though neither of them can stand the north wind. Lots of marriages are heading into north winds. It is vital to discern the truth of one's own mind, and then to speak it. Otherwise, you find out years later that you are in a situation that neither of you wanted in the first place.

Projection and the Inner Marriage

MW Projection is what brings people together. Projection is unconscious and projection is essential. There is no way of knowing ourselves without projections. To know what your inner world is, and who the inner beloved is, you first project that out onto a partner. Ultimately, you will have to realize that the partner is a human being and not the god or goddess that you are projecting. Then you may say, 'But I know my perfect beloved exists somewhere.' So you may leave the first person and carry on seeking this wonderful creature. And again you find someone to project upon; and again, maybe five or six times. Eventually, you get the message that these lovers are the same person you are falling in love with each time, and that the lover must have something to do with you. You can begin to see what you are projecting. Then you can say to yourself, 'This is my inner god and I am projecting; I will love him in my inner world, and perhaps a real man in the outer.'

Now, I do believe that if and when you find the man, you need a certain amount of projection going on, otherwise you are not in love. If you come to this level of awareness, you can choose. You can say, 'Yes, I'm going to jump over the cliff.' Or you can say, 'No, I'm not going to jump over the cliff. I've had enough of that. I don't want it any more.' Projection is life. It is desire. There is no desire without projection, nothing to reach out to. It's your love of beauty that makes you desire flowers in your house.

RH Can you say more about the relationship to the 'inner god' you were referring to?

MW Usually, a woman is projecting her own masculinity onto a man, and expects him to carry that aspect of herself; the man is usually expecting her to carry his femininity. Many old marriages were based on this traditional idea of relationship. In a mature relationship, both have developed the differentiated masculine and feminine in themselves, and they relate to each other from that differentiated place. One may be in the feminine, and responded to by the masculine in the other; or they may both be in their masculinity or their femininity. The point is that both these energies are in balance in a mature person. When you are just learning to carry both sides in yourself it can be quite exhausting. Although there is much more energy available, it is tempting to exploit that energy and burn the candle at both ends. Trying to live your mothering, your career and your lover nature all to the full in a relationship with a partner who is trying to do the same thing can be simply overwhelming. The physical body can't carry it all. As you become more used to it, you can carry it more lightly. In the world we live in, the slower rhythms of the feminine are in constant danger of being overrun.

After years of inner work, you may be blessed with the inner bridegroom or the inner bride. Then the inner marriage is in place, and you don't project that desire for perfection outwardly. You are then free to love a human being without archetypal projections. Neither you nor your partner needs to be a god or a goddess. The human relationship is free to be a human relationship. At the same time the inner marriage brings a profound sense of wholeness. It is very important to understand this, because when projection ceases, the partner may say, 'Well, you don't need me any more.' The truth is, they *don't* need the partner any more, and that leaves both free to really love.

This, I think, is where detachment comes in. By detachment

I do not mean indifference. I think that indifference is the end of a relationship. So long as people are fighting, they are still in relationship because they care enough to fight and put the energy into it. Once they no longer care about fighting, the indifference is in place and usually that is the end. Detachment, however, is recognizing the other person and recognizing yourself; it is allowing the other person to live their own life without the subjective claws that would hold on. Detachment holds one foot in and one foot out. It allows destiny to work through you, so that you are totally involved in life at the same time as allowing something else to be lived through you.

RH There is something larger than the personal will involved at that level, isn't there?

CG That's grace.

MW Yes, that's grace. That comes out of years of loving. Detachment comes out of years of loving. I suppose it could happen in new relationships when both persons have reached that level. I've never known a couple where that happened, though I suppose it could. I've known priests who've fallen in love with nuns and they felt that they'd reached that level of detachment. But when they actually started relating at a human level, they lost it. It is one thing to work it through in the imagination; it is quite another to work it through in experience.

RH It sounds like you are pointing to detachment as being the real marriage of those two myths we mentioned earlier: the myth of the individual journey and the myth of romantic love.

MW I think that if you are really on your individual path you do have to surrender your individual will. You have to recognize destiny working through you and you have to learn to co-operate with that. Hopefully, your partner thinks that way too or there's going to be one terrible clash at some point. The partner is going to think that you're a selfish bitch or selfish bastard or whatever. In romantic love it is a totally subjective attachment to each other. You are the one for me. In my experience of romantic love, each is projecting the inner divine and falling in love with the inner divine as it is projected onto the partner. Both hang on to that subjectivity. Detachment, on the other hand, is being able to separate from that subjectivity and bring in the objectivity of yourself and the other person.

CG For me, that detachment gave birth to my individuality, which was a vital requirement for our on-going relationship.

MW I would agree with that. There is the paradox. It happens when we can step back and see ourselves as part of the human comedy. We learn to love and let go.

RH It sounds like we might be discarding the whole notion of the soul mate as the illusion that accompanies projection.

MW I am not sure about that. We can't forget that it is the archetypal energy that is fundamental in relationship. You can rationally decide that person's got money, that person's good-looking, that person is right for me. That, though, wouldn't really be a marriage at all. Marriage has an archetypal dimension where we are working out our flaws, our gifts, what we have inherited, and what is unique in us. So a real soul mate is not the perfect partner, in the sense of being there to give us just what we want. We often have to fight hard with our soul mate because that person may appear to be the very obstacle to our becoming who we are. Precisely because they are the obstacle, they make us strong; and that is how they become our true soul mate. If you had a terrifically negative mother and you therefore marry a woman with a big power drive, you have to be a strong man to overcome that. Similarly, if the woman has a positive father and she marries a positive father who seems to be a perfect soul mate, she's going to have to really fight to get out of her infantile response to that man. She is going to be a *woman* when she has worked that relationship through. Moreover, he'll be a man, instead of a daddy. The archetypal dimension that is functioning there will hold two people together if they really get into it. I think there are some people strong enough to carry an archetypal projection without being destroyed by inflation. In my experience, I have found it once in my life. That one person had the kind of fire necessary to help me work it through.

CG When a couple has arrived at the detachment we were speaking of, what is there to keep them together?

MW If you have managed to develop the integration of masculinity and femininity in yourself . . . if and when that circuit is total, then it is also totally open. A couple in that situation is able to offer their love to the world in some form. I would also say that we are human beings, and most of us as human beings value companionship. Certainly, things happen in every encounter with someone that we love, and we discover new areas of ourselves. By love I mean an energy that is actually vibrant between people. If that vibration is cut off, the cells of the body change. You can tell in people who are not loved that there is a lack of frequency around the body. You can see this in older people who are rarely touched; and as soon as you touch them there is a difference in the vitality of the body. I think that this vibration which passes between two people changes them. Love transforms.

The Alchemical Wedding

MW The forging of an inner marriage in an individual is the work of building a subtle body; the subtle marriage is a union of two subtle bodies, a bonding of two souls. One or the other person may not even really want the bonding, but there is something so deep that, wherever one is, the other is aware of the other's psychic state, without any telephone. There is a recognition in the very cells of the body as to what is happening in the other person. The growth process occurring in one person on one continent will be affecting the growth process of the other, perhaps on a totally different plane of activity. Each could be physically married to another partner, but that connection is unbreakable. It is very hard for the marriage partner to accept that. Often, it simply has to be accepted, because it is part of destiny.

RH How could one distinguish between what one felt to be a subtle marriage and what might in actuality be a massive projection?

MW A very good question. I would say that you can work on integrating a projection, understanding it, and taking it off the other person; and yet this work does not change the subtle bond. With a projection you are yearning for the other; in a subtle marriage the other is already present with you wherever you are. In projection, there is a desire to possess in some way; the subtle relationship simply *is*. But this is a rare gift. You cannot make it happen, or pretend that it 'is'. Love chooses us.

The subtle marriage within the actual marriage is a rare thing. I have known people who met in early life, where the bond was made, and came back together at the end of their lives. They went through the development stages of life apart, and through letters or occasional meetings they developed the inner wholeness with each other. Then they came together at the end of their lives.

With the person you live with, there is always the tendency to rely on the other for the manifestation of your own opposite inner pole, or whatever aspect your partner is carrying for you. It does not feel so necessary to have to carry those aspects for yourself. If the other is not present, however, you have to do the work. Dante and Beatrice are an example. The imagination is profoundly involved in this, which is not, of course, to say that it is not real, or that it is just fantasy. It is not fantasy at all. The imagination is creating all the time, but if you are with the person, you are not using the imagination in the same way.

What we are really speaking of here is the alchemical wedding; and remember that the alchemical relationship is between the mystical brother and sister. If this were to occur in a marriage, I would think it would happen late in a couple's life, because it implies the total integration of lust and love. And that, perhaps above anything, is an almighty task!

FINAL THOUGHTS

Stirring the oatmeal is a humble act – not exciting or thrilling. But it symbolizes a relatedness that brings love down to earth . . . Love is content to do many things that ego is bored with. Love is willing to work with the other person's moods and unreasonableness. Love is willing to fix breakfast and balance the checkbook. Love is willing to do these 'oatmeal' things of life because it is related to a person, not a projection.

Human love sees another person as an individual and makes an individualized relationship to him or her. Romantic love sees the other person only as a role player in the drama.

A man's human love desires that a woman become a complete and independent person and encourages her to be herself. Romantic love only affirms what he would like her to be, so that she could be identical to anima. So long as romance rules a man, he affirms a woman only insofar as she is willing to change, so that she may reflect his projected ideal. Romance is never happy with the other person just as he or she is.

From *We: Understanding the Psychology of Romantic Love*
by ROBERT A. JOHNSON

Love is an action, an activity. Love is not a feeling . . . the person who truly loves does so because of a decision to love. This person has made a commitment to be loving whether or not the loving feeling is present. True love is not a feeling by which we are overwhelmed. It is a committed, thoughtful decision.

From *The Road Less Travelled* (Rider, 1978)
by M. SCOTT PECK

Without shame people will boast that they have loved, do love or hope to love. As if love were enough, or could cover any multitude of sins. But love, as we have seen, when it is not conscious love – that is to say, love that aims to be both wise and able in the service of its object – is either an affinity or a dis-affinity, and in both cases equally unconscious, that is, uncontrolled. To be in such a state of love is to be dangerous either to oneself or to the other or to both. We are then polarized to a natural force (which has its own objects to serve regardless of ours) and charged with its force; and events are fortunate if we do not damage somebody in consequence of carrying dynamite carelessly. Love without knowledge and power is demoniac. Without knowledge it may destroy the beloved. Who has not seen many a beloved made wretched and ill by her or his 'lover'? Without power the lover must become wretched, since he cannot do for his beloved what he wishes and knows to be for her delight. Men should pray to be spared the experience of love without wisdom and strength. Or, finding themselves in love, they should pray for knowledge and power to guide their love. Love is *not* enough.

From *On Love* (James Press, 1974) by A. R. ORAGE.

The 'I' and the 'we' is not a case of either/or but of both/and. I am uniquely me, something in myself that only I can be, and I am also my relationships with others, something larger than myself. To transcend this tension between the I and the not-I, we need to ground the reality of 'we' in a new conceptual structure which gives equal weight to individuals and to their relationships, a structure which rests on the physics of consciousness. We need to see how it is, physically, that 'we' can be both a compound of 'I' and 'you' *and* a new thing in itself with its own qualities. Such composite individuals are not possible in classical physics, but we know that they are the norm in quantum physics.

This new conceptual structure for interpersonal relations can be found in the tensions within the wave/particle duality and the ability of an elementary particle to be both a wave and a particle simulotaneously.

From *The Quantum Self* (Flamingo, 1990) by DANA ZOHAR.

That love can change its face so quickly from angelic bliss to fiendish spitefulness results from its being founded on our woundedness. On the one hand, we are never so complete and so satisfied as when we are with the individual whose being and whose wound corresponds to our own. On the other hand, one one else is so capable of ripping open that wound as the one to whom we have given our heart.

From *Divine Madness: Archetypes of Romantic Love* (Shambhala, 1990) by JOHN R. HAULE.

To take love seriously and to bear and to learn it like a task, this it is that young people need. Like so much else, people have also misunderstood the place of love in life, they have made it into play and pleasure because they thought that play and pleasure were more blissful than words, but there is nothing happier than work, and love, just because it is the extreme happiness, can be nothing but work. So whoever loves must try to act as if he had a great work: he must be much alone and go into himself and collect himself and hold fast to himself; he must work; he must become something!

For believe me, the more one is, the richer is all that one experiences. And whoever wants to have a deep love in his life must collect and save for it and gather honey.

From *Rilke on Love and Other Difficulties: Translations and Considerations of Rainer Maria Rilke* (Norton & Co., 1975) by JOHN J. L. MOOD.

When a man wants a woman to live for him alone, and a woman wants a man to live for her alone . . . and when this is called true love . . . it is true love condemned to perish before long. When a man and a woman, together, open up to others – when the man can find joy in feeling that his wife goes towards others with love, and the woman can find joy in feeling that her husband goes towards others with love – then the couple is destined to grow, then it can no longer be ravaged by emotions.

From *Towards The Fullness of Life* (Threshold Books, 1990) by ARNAUD DESJARDINS.

A Third Body

A man and a woman sit near each other, and they do
    not long
at this moment to be older, or younger, nor born
in any other nation, or time, or place.
They are content to be where they are, talking or
    not-talking.
Their breaths together feed someone whom we do
    not know.
The man sees the way his fingers move;
he sees her hands close around a book she hands
    to him.
They obey a third body that they share in common.
They have made a promise to love that body.
Age may come, parting may come, death will come.
A man and a woman sit near each other;
as they breathe they feed someone we do not know,
someone we know of, whom we have never seen.

From the collection *Loving a Woman in Two Worlds*
by ROBERT BLY

NOTES ON CONTRIBUTORS

Robert Ansell, born, bred, trained and experienced as a criminal trial lawyer, reincarnated without changing bodies at the age of 38. This tremendously cost-effective technique enabled him to pursue life anew as a father, husband, musician, photographer, and producer.

Terry Cooper is 41 years old, a psychotherapist and trainer in psychotherapy. In 1976 he co-founded Spectrum, a centre for humanistic psychology in London, England, where he currently practises. His special areas of interest are working with couples, running men's workshops and long intensive residential courses. Terry lives with his wife, Jenner, his son, Jodie, two Irish setters called Kit and Lara, and Romeo and Juliet – a pair of love birds – and their four eggs.

Riane Eisler is co-founder of the Centre for Partnership Studies, a founding member of the General Evolution Research Group, and a consultant to corporations working in the media and the arts, including Paramount Pictures and Disney Imagineering. She is the author of *The Chalice and the Blade: Our History, Our Future*. This book, which has been translated into 10 languages, identifies the partnership and dominator models as two basic choices for our species.

Chloe Goodchild is a singer, voice teacher, and mother of Rebecca. Sound, sensuality and silence are at the heart of her life and work. She has produced two albums, *Inner Heat* and *The Voice Inside Her*, which are innovative in bridging Eastern and Western vocal styles. Her book *Being and the Voice Inside Her* is being published by Random Century in 1993.

Christopher Greatorex had his first birthday at about the same time as the outbreak of the Second World War, but has yet to discover the significance of the synchronicity. He has changed career three times, having started as an actor, followed by 15 years in the hotel business, 10 of which were spent on a smallholding in Oxfordshire where he had his own restaurant. In the wake of his cancer diagnosis in 1978, he trained as an acupuncturist and psychotherapist, and now practises in Stroud with individuals, couples and groups. His interest in holistic and humanistic medicine sparked off a programme of courses, Medical Synthesis, designed to support health professionals, in particular those in the field of life-threatening illness.

Frances Greatorex trained at Camberwell Art School in the 1960s. She then found an equally creative pursuit in embracing marriage and childrearing for the next 25 years. This proved to be the perfect training ground for her work as a painter. Painting is not only her creative self-expression, it has become a means of transformation and spiritual discipline. She now divides her time between her studio and her home and relationship, finding that they enhance and complement each other. Out of this experience together, Frances and Christopher run workshops on Partnership, which they feel to be one of the biggest challenges of our time. For information on these workshops, write to F. and C. Greatorex, Leaways, Downend, Horsley, Glos. GL6 0PQ.

Roger Housden runs the Open Gate Conference Programme and organizes 'inner journeys' to India and the Sahara Desert. He is moved by travel, writing, photography and perennial questions. The son of a lorry driver, Roger was born in London in 1945 and grew up in Bath. He now lives in Bristol. His book *Fire in the Heart* was published by Element Books in 1990. His forthcoming book *The Soul is in the Senses* will be published by Random Century in 1993.

Eve Penner Ilsen studied with Joseph Campbell, then began her long training as a pioneer in therapeutic bodymind work. She received a degree in psychology, and studied imagery and the waking dream extensively. A singer, story-teller, psychotherapist and graduate-level teacher, she works with Reb Zalman on retreats, seminars, and in creating the Wisdom School.

David Loye is a social psychologist, futurist, and systems theorist. He is the author of major books on the use of the brain and mind in prediction, political leadership, race relations, and is the developer of a new theory of moral sensitivity. His psycho-history *The Healing of a Nation* received the Anisfield-Wolfe Award for the best scholarly book on race relations in 1971. His book *The Sphinx and the Rainbow: Brain, Mind, and Future Vision* has been translated into five languages. Loye is co-director of The Centre for Partnership Studies, and a founding member of the General Evolution Research Group.

Peter Redgrove read science at Cambridge, has worked as a research scientist and scientific journalist, and is regarded as one of the country's leading poets. He has published 19 books of verse, seven novels, and is well known as a playwright, having won the Italia Prize in 1982. He trained as a lay analyst with Dr John Layard during 1968–9, and is co-author with Penelope Shuttle of *The Wise Wound*. His study of visionary states, *The Black Goddess*, appeared in 1987.

Gabrielle Roth is a noted theatre director, dance teacher and shamanic healer. She has devoted her life to exploring and communicating the language of primal movement, ecstatic experience and the journey of the soul. Author of *Maps to*

Ecstasy: Teachings of an Urban Shaman, she is the Artistic Director of her dance/theatre/music company, The Mirrors, and has been a member of The Artist's Studio (Director's Unit). Her music tapes, including *Waves, Ritual, Bones, Initiation*, and *Totem*, are at the cutting edge of shamanic trance/dance music.

Jenner Roth is a Founder Director and working Director of Spectrum, a centre for humanistic psychology in London. She is the creator of the Spectrum Sexuality Programme and Chair of the Spectrum Incest Intervention Project. She has been instrumental in the introduction of humanistic psychology to the UK and Europe. She was Director of Center in Amsterdam from 1972 to 1976. Jenner's particular therapeutic interest is in developing and teaching observational skills. She maintains a private practice in London. She is married to Terry Cooper and they have a son, Jodie.

Rabbi Zalman Schachter is founder of the P'nai Or Wisdom School and is at the forefront of Jewish Spiritual Renewal in the United States. His particular contribution has been to expand on the traditional teachings of the Kabbalah and Hasidism, and to bring his wide knowledge of other spiritual traditions to bear on his teaching of Jewish spirituality. His published works include *The First Step: a Guide to the New Jewish Spirit*; *Fragments of a Future Scroll*; *Sparks of Light* and *The Dream Assembly*.

Eileen Scott taught biological sciences before switching to industry where she became head of the research and consultancy services in the agricultural subsidiary of ICI. She then moved to marketing, and subsequently introduced strategic planning to the company, which she headed until the early 1980s. After leaving industry she acquired skills in a wide range of methods of creativity and self-awareness, and has recently become a professional sculptress and painter. She comes from a Celtic family with a long history, which has given her the sense of a memory that stretches back through time.

Michael Scott served in the RAF and then worked in research and consultancy. He became chief executive of a company where his main objective was to lead that company through fundamental change using strategic perspectives to manage people and other resources. He was a member of the CBI central committee for industrial policy. In 1987 he became a freelance consultant, and now combines his dedication to the ideals of self-development and creativity as a professional painter with his managerial expertise. He and Eileen Scott run groups together in York on creativity and self-awareness.

Penelope Shuttle was born in Middlesex in 1947, and now lives in Cornwall with husband Peter Redgrove and daughter Zoe. She has published poetry and novels, and has a new collection of verse, *Taxing the Rain*, in preparation for 1992 publication. She has collaborated with Peter Redgrove on two novels and a book of verse, but their major work together is the pioneer study, *The Wise Wound*, a psychological study of the menstrual cycle, first published in 1978, reissued by Grafton Books in 1986.

Marion Woodman is a Jungian analyst in private practice in Toronto. The author of several books, including *Addiction to Perfection* (1982), *The Pregnant Virgin* (1985) and *The Ravaged Bridgegroom* (1990), she is one of North America's leading Jungian writers and workshop presenters.